Kidnapped by Accident

Illustrated by **Victor G. Ambrus**

Weekly Reader Children's Book Club

presents

Kidnapped by Accident

by Arthur Catherall

Lothrop, Lee & Shepard Co., New York

Also by Arthur Catherall

LAPLAND OUTLAW
NIGHT OF THE BLACK FROST
PRISONERS IN THE SNOW
SICILIAN MYSTERY
THE STRANGE INTRUDER
YUGOSLAV MYSTERY

Weekly Reader Children's Book Club Edition
Senior Division

Contents

The Red Dolphin

1

IF THE SHOAL OF HERRING had not suddenly swum near to the surface of the sea, Mikael Ekman and his sister would never have seen the *Red Dolphin*. Fourteen-year-old Mikael and thirteen-year-old Marjatta were walking along the island beach toward their small boat. Their father Juhan had just said that they must row back to their home, which was on another island, because he and the fishermen with him were going to try their luck farther out in the Baltic.

Then, quite suddenly, sea birds began streaking from all directions toward a patch of water less than a quarter of a mile away. The Baltic was as smooth as a lake, for the day was calm, with only occasional puffs of light, warm wind. It was just the right kind of day for a holiday, even for swimming, though the water off the southwest coast of Finland never gets very warm.

Even from the quarter-of-a-mile distance the fishermen could hear the excited squawking of the sea birds as they dived down, to rise a few seconds later with small Baltic herring, known as strömming, in their beaks. Juhan Ekman and his fisherman friends did not waste a moment. Three of them jumped into a boat and began to tow out their long, fine-meshed net.

For most of the men who live in the maze of islands which lie between Finland and the coast of Sweden, the herring provides bread and butter. The fishermen were excited now, for the water was flecked with white where the fish were leaping out into the sunshine. It looked like a record shoal of strömming. With luck they might earn a week's wages in a few hours!

The men in the boat would tow their long line of netting out, swing it around the seaward side of the shoal, then row in a half circle back to the shore. When that was done, the entire shoal would be enclosed by the netting like a wall. Cork floats held up its top and its bottom was weighted. Not many herring would escape once the boat had rowed between the shoal and the open sea.

On shore Mikael, Marjatta, their father Juhan, and another fisherman waited in silence. They watched the men in the boat row almost to the point where the shoal would be trapped. Then, for some unknown reason, the strömming stopped swimming toward the shore. Despite all the men could do, more than half the shoal managed to escape back to the open sea.

"Don't worry," Juhan Ekman said, stroking Marjatta's coal-black hair. "We never cry over lost fish. What we do not catch today we may catch tomorrow. Now, off you go. While you are rowing home, Mikael, Marjatta can be preparing the herring for curing. And when you get home you can find enough oak for the curing fires."

"If we had got that shoal we would have had a catch to make us rich," Mikael muttered regretfully.

"We Finns never get rich," his father said, clapping a hand on Mikael's shoulder. "If we were rich we would stop working. Then we would grow lazy and fat. Marjatta, tell Mother I shall not be home until tomorrow night. Even if we missed the big catch, there will be enough fish here to make a trip to Turku market worthwhile. Here, you had better take my small knife. It isn't easy to clean fish without a good knife." He handed his daughter the knife, then turned to lend a hand at pulling in the big net.

"One of these days I'll clean the fish and you can row," Mikael grumbled.

Marjatta immediately held out the small knife. "I'll row and you clean the fish," she challenged. She smiled when Mikael shook his head. She knew he preferred rowing any time to cleaning fish. Together they walked along to their small dinghy, bright with new paint.

The island where the Ekman family lived was about three miles from where the men had chosen to fish, but Juhan Ekman was not the least worried as his children pushed their boat out into deep water. Three times a week they had to row to another island to go to school, so Mikael and Marjatta were almost as much at home in a boat as on land. After watching Mikael begin to row, Juhan Ekman turned to help haul in the laden net.

Three hundred yards out, the sea birds were still flying excitedly over the water where the shoal of herring were now heading for deeper water. The flashing wings

caught the sunlight, as did the foam thrown up when the
birds dived into the quiet sea. It was a picture of peace—
with a red-painted yacht on the skyline sailing nearer
and nearer.

In the small boat Marjatta was soon busy cleaning the
fish. When she and her brother reached their island they
would hang the herring up on racks in a shed built for
this purpose. Mikael would light a fire of oak chips under
them. The smoke from the fire would quietly climb the
racks, and after a time the herring would turn a pale

golden color. Smoked, or cured in this way, they could be kept for a long time. For the Ekman family, and for most of the people of the islands, smoked herring was the main item for many a meal during the long, hard winter.

For half an hour, while Marjatta worked busily with her knife, her brother rowed with tireless ease. He was whistling softly to himself, lost in thought, until the red-painted yacht came so close that he could not help seeing it.

"Look behind you, Marjatta," he said, resting for a moment on his oars. "How would you like a boat like that? Isn't she a beauty? I wonder who owns her."

A herring in one hand and the knife in the other, Marjatta swiveled around in her seat in the stern and looked at the yacht. It was a lovely, graceful craft. Painted a rich red, its tall mast gleamed a pale gold in the sunlight. The sails were all furled, except one tiny sail in the stern, and the vessel was moving under the power of an engine. They could hear the steady *thrum-thrum-thrum* and see the foam the propeller was kicking up at the stern.

"Do you remember the British yachtsman who bought fish from us last year?" Marjatta asked, an excited gleam in her eyes. "He gave us some chocolate. I wonder if this yacht is British. I . . . what's that in the bow? It's a red fish, over the name place. Can you read the name?"

"I think it's a Swedish yacht," Mikael said. "The name is in Swedish, I'm sure. Oh, I'll bet I know the name. That painted fish is a red dolphin."

"I'm going to see if they'd like some herring." Cupping her hands about her mouth, Marjatta sent a shrill call ringing out across the almost waveless water. "Hello . . . hello . . . would you like some fish?"

"You shouldn't do that," Mikael protested rather crossly. "It's like begging. They'll probably buy some fish because they think we're poor, and . . . oh, a dog. Someone is coming on deck."

A small black-and-white fox terrier had suddenly appeared in the stern of the yacht and was barking furiously. He kept this up for a few moments, then disappeared. By this time the *Red Dolphin* was within sixty yards of the Ekman boat.

A sudden puff of wind had filled the little sail at the stern of the yacht and at once it changed course. Mikael understood this; he had heard of automatic steering, in which a small sail in the stern worked the tiller and the rudder.

Suddenly, when the yacht was no more than fifty yards away, a hand appeared through a porthole not far from the bow. Mikael and Marjatta gazed in amazement at something being waved to and fro, as if someone were signaling to them. It seemed to be burning; it blazed and gave off thick smoke.

Then the hand was withdrawn. A moment later they saw a face framed in the tiny porthole and heard a man shout: "Hello, can you help me? I'm trapped in the forward cabin. Could you come aboard, please." At almost the same moment the fox terrier reappeared at the stern. Barking in great excitement, he seemed to be trying to tell the two young Finns that his master needed help.

Marjatta pushed her knife into the sheath at her waist. Mikael grabbed the oars and spun the boat around. He looked anxiously for some rope-ends hanging over the yacht's side which he could grab as they slid alongside.

Two things went wrong. Mikael had never before tried to come alongside a moving vessel and he did not realize that the yacht was sliding through the water at about six miles an hour. The second thing was another puff of wind from the west which filled the little sail at the stern. Because it was working a mechanical steering mechanism, it swung the helm over.

The *Red Dolphin* was not only a lovely yacht to look at, but it answered its helm as swiftly and easily as a well-trained pony answers the touch of a rein. As the rudder was pushed over by the automatic steering, the yacht heeled slightly and turned. One moment it was sliding through the water in a direction which would have taken it just past Mikael and his sister in their small boat. The next moment it was turning, and the long, varnished bowsprit seemed to be charging at them like the lance of a mounted Hussar.

Marjatta screamed to her brother to row, but Mikael knew there was no time.

"Jump, Marja, JUMP!" he roared. For a split second he held back, knowing that if they both tried to dive at once from the same side their tiny craft might turn over. As soon as he saw his sister dive, he dived. And he was not an instant too soon.

Mikael heard the *crunch* as the bow of the *Red*

Dolphin smashed the planking of their little boat. He could also hear something else—a menacing *thump-thump-thump*. It was the yacht's propeller churning up the water as it turned, and drawing anything at hand into its gleaming bronze blades.

Fear for his sister made Mikael forget his own peril. He spread his arms in a swift stroke that turned him to one side so that he could look for Marjatta.

The sea was full of bubbles, and the sunlight shone down through the water, turning it a golden green. To his right the red hull of the yacht was sliding past, and he could see the great keel which held it upright when the sails were spread.

Out of the corner of his eye as he looked for Marjatta, he caught a glimpse of their battered little boat. It was being rolled over and over under the keel of the yacht, almost as if the *Red Dolphin* were deliberately trying to smash it to matchwood.

Now Mikael caught sight of his sister. She had dived quite deep and was rising, bubbles streaming up from her dark hair. He reached out, grasped her hand, and kicked mightily with his legs. Together they bobbed to the surface like corks.

Nearby was an oar, Marjatta's woolen cap, an up-turned fish box, and a small reel of greased fishing line. As the stern of the *Red Dolphin* swept by, Marjatta and Mikael saw a dinghy being towed along from the yacht's stern. It was painted as red as the yacht, and it bobbed merrily in the churned-up foam thrown to the surface by the yacht's propeller.

"Grab . . . grab the dinghy!" Mikael tried to shout, but a tiny wave slopped into his face, filling his throat with water and making him choke.

Marjatta needed no urging. She was hampered by the woolen frock she was wearing, which was already heavy with water. She gave a despairing cry—"I can't do it!"— but even as she spoke she was plunging through the water with a frantic breast stroke which took her to the dinghy just in time.

Mikael followed. He grabbed the gunwale, and his free arm went around his sister. An instant later he gasped with pain as the jolt almost broke his hold on the dinghy, which was being towed along by the *Red Dolphin*. The yacht was moving through the water at close to six miles an hour, hauling Mikael and Marjatta and the little boat along at the same speed.

"Grab with both hands," he spluttered. Marjatta obeyed, and Mikael was able to take his arm from around her and get a firmer grip on the dinghy's stern.

Anyone who had not spent as much time as Mikael and Marjatta in boats might easily have been lost. The speed which drew them to the surface was hard on the arm muscles. But doing so much rowing, as well as hard work about the house and little farm, had made them much stronger than most children of their age. They hung on for a moment, getting back their breath. Then Mikael gasped: "Hold on, Marja. I'm going to try and climb over the stern. Then I'll help you in. Are you all right?"

Marjatta nodded. Nerving himself for the effort,

Mikael dragged himself close up to the stern of the dinghy. It kept bobbing up and down, as if it had a demon in it who was determined to shake off the two young Finns and leave them to drown.

As the dinghy bobbed down, after what seemed a higher than usual upward heave, Mikael made his try. Calling on his arm and shoulder muscles for a mighty effort, he heaved upward. A moment later he was lying half across the stern, half in the water. Had he not been worried about Marjatta he would have remained that way for a minute or so to get back his strength, but he was afraid for his sister.

Still coughing from the sea water he had swallowed, he wormed his way over the stern, then turned to help Marjatta. He could tell by her tightly closed lips that she was very near the end of her strength. Wasting no breath on words, he leaned over, grabbed her arms, waited until the dinghy dipped its stern, then yelled: "Up . . . UP . . . UP!"

Seconds later Mikael was rolling back into the bottom

of the dinghy and Marjatta was sprawled over the stern with her legs dangling in the water, exactly as he had been a minute or so earlier. Without any more help from her brother she dragged herself inboard. Then she flopped face down, her chest heaving as she fought for breath.

Only five or six minutes had passed since the terrifying moment when the bow of the *Red Dolphin* had swung around and the yacht had charged for their boat. In those few minutes Mikael and Marjatta had used up all their strength. Now they were too winded and exhausted to do anything but lie and gasp for air.

The dinghy bobbed less wildly now, with the weight of the two children to hold it down. The *thrum-thrum-thrum* of the yacht's powerful engine was almost like a lullaby to Marjatta. She lay with her face turned sideways, resting on her hands, which kept her cheek from touching the bottom boards of the dinghy. She filled and refilled her lungs, wondering if she would ever have the strength to move again.

Mikael felt the same way. His shoulders ached as if he had spent a whole day swinging a felling ax among the dwarf oaks and junipers on their island. His lungs were crying out for air, and he kept coughing and spluttering to get rid of the water he had swallowed. Had the sea been as salty as ordinary seas he might have been sick, but the Baltic is only slightly salty—since it is almost an inland sea, without tides.

It was the dog that finally forced Mikael to sit up. How long he had been lying face down in the dinghy he

did not know, but as the shrill barking went on and on
he got to his knees. The black-and-white terrier was
standing in the stern of the *Red Dolphin,* staring anxiously at the bobbing dinghy.

The moment Mikael got to his knees the barking be-
came even more insistent. He saw the dog leap into the
well of the yacht and rush to the door of the cabin.
There it stopped and barked again, pleadingly, as if trying to coax Mikael to come and look at something.

Mikael, however, was not even thinking about the dog.
As he got to his knees he looked around, as any sailor
will, to see where they were. For a moment or so he
stared, perplexed. Then he gasped. They were moving
steadily toward an island. They had passed the island
where he and Marjatta lived, and were heading for one
of the most dangerous places he knew.

Turning, he shook his sister. "Marja . . . MARJA . . .
wake up!" he shouted. "We're heading for Jorholmeer,
MARJA . . . get up, quick! We'll be on the rocks in a
minute."

The word *Jorholmeer* shook Marjatta out of her sleepy
state. The strain of the few minutes in the water had
taken all her strength, but the word *Jorholmeer* would
waken any island Finn. No one lived on Jorholmeer, for
it was almost impossible to land on that island. It was
guarded by scores of rocks, most of them barely covered
with water. It was so dangerous that a small, automatic
lighthouse had been placed on one rock to warn sailors
at night not to come too close.

"Hurry up," Mikael urged, trying to get his sister to

her knees. "If we hit a rock we'll sink in no time, and you know how dangerous it is here."

Marjatta did know, and the thought drove the sleepiness out of her eyes at once. With Mikael steadying her against the rocking of the dinghy she stood up and looked. The island's rock-cluttered approach was very near now; their only chance was to try to get the yacht moving on another course.

Both she and Mikael had worked on boats long enough to know what they had to do. Scrambling toward the front of the dinghy, they grasped the rope which went from the bow of the little craft to the stern of the yacht. If they pulled hard enough on this line they could haul the dinghy up to the larger vessel.

"When we're close enough, you jump aboard and put the tiller hard over," Mikael ordered, as he heaved on the connecting rope. Alone, he would never have managed to pull the little craft near enough, for the pluck of the water as they forged along was very strong. But with both of them pulling with all their strength, they began to haul themselves nearer the *Red Dolphin*.

As if he knew they needed encouragement, the little fox terrier was now back at the stern of the yacht, yapping excitedly and even wagging his stumpy tail. Once, in his eagerness, he almost fell into the sea. But the moment he recovered he began to yap shrilly and wag his tail.

Mikael and Marjatta hauled the dinghy closer and closer until finally the two craft were bumping together.

"NOW!" Mikael panted, hanging on desperately.

He was certain he would not be able to hold the dinghy close for more than a few seconds, once Marjatta's help had gone.

Despite her wet clothes and her fatigue, Marjatta scrambled past Mikael, grabbed the polished brass rail which ran around the *Red Dolphin's* stern, heaved herself off the dinghy's bow, and scrambled over the low rail. As she did this, Mikael was forced to let go the rope because the strain was so great he felt as if his arms were breaking.

The moment he stopped pulling on the rope the dinghy was swept backward. When the slack was taken up on the rope there was a terrific *twang*, and the yacht began towing the smaller boat again. The jerk threw Mikael down, and he bumped his head on the center seat.

He sat up, rubbing the back of his head. At that instant something happened to the yacht. For a moment it seemed as if it had run into a stone wall. As its easy forward rush was halted, it heeled over to the left. Then, as the dinghy still rushed on, as if intent on crashing into the *Red Dolphin's* stern, the yacht seemed to shake itself, and with a shudder it moved forward again.

The dinghy rose on a small wave, then crashed down on the same hidden rock which had just jarred the yacht.

Crunch! Mikael winced at what felt like a tremendous hammer blow under the dinghy. Then he was moving once more as the line connecting the dinghy to the yacht tightened again.

The momentary grounding had done one good thing. It had changed the direction the yacht was taking. Now, instead of heading toward the rocky coastline of Jorholmeer Island, the *Red Dolphin* was heading gently out to sea again.

Mikael rubbed his shoulders and caressed the bump on the back of his head. At the same time he looked toward the yacht to see what his sister was doing. She was on her feet and appeared to be struggling with the small sail in the *Red Dolphin's* stern—the sail which controlled the steering of the yacht.

"Cut it free," Mikael yelled. "If you . . ." There he stopped. A sudden coolness on his legs made him look down. Startled, he saw that he was kneeling in more than an inch of water. It had not come over the sides of the dinghy, for the little boat was riding the waves as easily as a duck. The boat was leaking!

His hands felt about in the rising water, and he was shocked to feel two broken boards. When the dinghy had crashed down onto the hidden rock the impact had smashed part of the planking. Mikael knew at once the boat could not be kept afloat. Water was rushing in more quickly than anyone could bail it out.

He cupped his hands about his mouth and yelled his loudest. "Marja . . . MARJA! Stop the engine. I'm sinking." He saw his sister turn, stare, then leave the steering gear and drop out of sight into the well where the engine controls were. There was nothing he could do now but wait, and while he waited the water rose higher and higher.

The dinghy was no longer bobbing about like a playful duck but was dragging heavily through the water. The rope which connected it to the *Red Dolphin's* stern jerked ominously, and Mikael had a feeling that even the best rope would not be able to withstand that treatment for long. He splashed to the bow with the idea of taking some of the strain off the rope, but it was so taut that it felt like a bar of iron.

Then, to his horror, the rope gave a little jerk, and he saw that one of the strands had broken. Like two snakes the broken ends began to unravel, putting extra strain on the unbroken strands. Mikael knew much about ropes. Even as a seven-year-old he had sat at his father's knee, learning how to splice ropes and mend fishing nets. When one strand in a three-strand rope broke, the remaining strands would not last long. He yelled desperately and got no reply. Marjatta was out of sight, still trying to stop the engine. But the *thrum-thrum-thrum* went on and on.

A second strand broke, and for a few moments there was a sickening jerking of the rope as the one remaining strand tightened and slackened. Then it, too, snapped.

The *Red Dolphin* sailed on as if it never had been towing a dinghy, leaving Mikael kneeling in the slowly sinking boat. The water rose and rose until it was up to the gunwales, and then the dinghy slipped under. Mikael began to swim. But the moment his weight was off the dinghy the little boat came gently to the surface again. It would not sink to the bottom for a long time, for it was made of wood, and wood floats; but it would not bear Mikael's weight.

Mikael swam back to the dinghy. Hanging on, he shouted and shouted, but there was no reply. Even the little fox terrier was no longer barking. Both the dog and Marjatta were out of sight, and the *Red Dolphin* was making for the open sea. Steadily the gap between the yacht and its dinghy grew greater. A froth of white foam at its stern told Mikael that the engine was still thrumming away. A choking lump filled his throat.

A sea bird swooped down, on the lookout for food. Mikael lifted an arm to fend off a possible jab from a cruel yellow beak. The sea bird, squawking in sudden alarm, beat the air furiously with its powerful wings. That thing in the water was not a fish, but a human being.

Mikael struggled to drag off his sodden jacket. He was more than half a mile from Jorholmeer Island. There were dangerous hidden rocks between him and the cliffs, but if he did not want to drown, he would have to try to swim ashore.

Mystery Aboard the
Red Dolphin

2

ABOARD THE YACHT, Marjatta had no idea the rope connecting the dinghy to *Red Dolphin* had broken. She peered at the powerful diesel engine, wondering how it worked. There seemed to be only two levers, and when she timidly pushed at one of them the *thrum-thrum-thrum* of the engine rose to a sudden roar. She felt the yacht begin to tremble, and it heeled as it began to pick up speed.

Hastily she drew the lever back to its original position while the little dog watched her anxiously, his bright eyes filled with pleading, as if he wondered why she was here when he wanted her to come with him into the cabin. After a moment Marjatta pulled the lever back, and at once the *thrum-thrum-thrum* slowed down. She pulled it back as far as it would come, hoping the engine would stop; but it kept on, though it was now working rather jerkily.

"Well, anyway we're going slower now," she murmured. She got to her feet and climbed the three-runged ladder which led up to the deck, where the steering mechanism was. "I should be able to haul Mikael . . ."

and there her voice trailed off into horror-stricken silence.

There was no dinghy to be seen, and the sea between her and Jorholmeer Island seemed to be completely empty. She screamed, "Mikael! Mikael!" Within seconds she heard a faint answer, but it came from somewhere in the yacht: "Hello . . . hello . . . hello! Help! Help me!"

Marjatta turned, and the fox terrier, which had followed her into the stern, began to bark excitedly. Then she saw a distant sea bird, looking more like a fluttering piece of paper than a bird, drop down toward something on the water. Suddenly it rose up again with swiftly beating wings.

Marjatta had seen too many sea birds fishing not to

know what that quick winging up into the air meant. Whatever the bird had swooped down on was not food. "It's Mikael," she sobbed with relief. Turning, she tried to push the tiller over to turn the yacht around. She succeeded, but only with a great effort, for the tiller was still connected to the automatic steering mechanism which was worked by the small sail.

Marjatta drew out the knife her father had given her for cleaning the herring and slashed through two ropes, freeing the tiller. Quickly she pushed it hard over and was relieved to see the slow-moving yacht begin to turn about.

In the next few minutes Marjatta Ekman not only proved that she was a sailor, but that she could face trouble with courage. As the yacht was headed back toward the spot where the sea bird had swooped down, Marjatta slid down the three steps to the well deck, where the engine was located. She pushed the throttle lever forward without hesitation, and as the soft *thrum-thrum* changed to a swifter, more powerful beat, she hurried back to the tiller.

The dog began to bark again, and even tried to nip Marjatta's heels. Anxious and worried, she shouted angrily at him—and was sorry immediately. Bending, she stroked the frantic animal.

"I know . . . I know," she told him. "There's somebody in the cabin, and he's in trouble. I'll come—later. Later!" And she patted the dog's head.

The terrier looked up at her, his eyes bright with anxiety; yet he seemed to understand. His tail drooped, but he stopped barking and did not bother Marjatta again.

A few minutes later something splashed in the water a hundred yards distant. Until then she had searched the greeny-blue surface of the sea in vain for a sign of her brother. Like most people who spend a great deal of their time looking out over water, Marjatta had wonderful vision. Now she lifted her hands to her eyes, ringing thumbs and forefingers as if they were binoculars. This was an old sailor's trick, which enabled a person to look at just one small patch of sea or sky.

It worked immediately for Marjatta. She saw the splashing again, and within seconds was able to pick out her brother. She saw that he was swimming back to the waterlogged boat. From that moment she never took her eyes off him.

She steered the yacht around in a great circle. Then, as the *Red Dolphin* came closer to the half-sunken dinghy, Marjatta closed the engine throttle until the yacht was moving at only a little more than a mile an hour. Throwing a looped rope to Mikael, she began a tremendous struggle to help him aboard, but ten tiring minutes passed before the rescue was complete.

While the *Red Dolphin* chugged along at the slowest possible speed, Mikael sat with his back to the stern sail, his head bowed and water dripping from him. He was breathing heavily. Climbing aboard a moving vessel is not easy, even when the vessel is going very slowly.

"I couldn't get back to you any quicker," Marjatta apologized. "I'm sorry."

"You . . . got . . . back . . . that's all . . . that . . .
matters." Mikael stretched out a dripping hand to grasp
his sister's hand. "If . . . I . . . oh, go away. Go on!" He
was speaking to the dog which had got its teeth into the
bottom of his wet trouser leg and was tugging at it.

Marjatta remembered the man in the *Red Dolphin's*
cabin.

"I forgot! The man in the cabin. Should I—"

"I'll come with you." Mikael rose slowly and flicked
his hands to free them of the water running down his
arms. "As soon as we've seen to him, we're turning this
yacht around and heading for home as fast as she'll go.
Dry clothes and a hot drink is what we both need."

Marjatta nodded and ran her fingers through her
damp hair, brushing it off her forehead and pushing the
side fringes behind her ears. The terrier, whining anxiously, was already down in the well deck, standing in
front of the cabin door.

"The man shouted to me," Marjatta explained, following her brother down the three steps. "But I didn't have
time to go in. I'd just discovered that the dinghy had
broken away. Oh, Mikael, do you think we should have
tried to get it back?"

"The dinghy? It's too late now." Mikael pushed his
dripping hair away from his eyes. Walking into the cabin
he called, "Hello . . . hello!" Then he stopped and looked
down, for he was splashing in several inches of water.
Marjatta was equally startled, but before they could
comment on the water there was a call from the forward
cabin.

"Hello . . . hello. Can you help me? I'm stuck here. I can't open the cabin door."

The cabin was about twelve feet long and about nine feet wide, with lockers on each side and a folding table stacked neatly on top of the right-hand lockers. Everything suggested that the owner of the yacht was a man of wealth. The wall-to-wall carpet, though now covered with two inches of water, was thick and richly colored.

The door dividing this cabin from the forward one was a sliding one. Mikael pressed down on the chromium-plated handle and pulled, but the door refused to move.

"Is there a lock?" Marjatta called.

"A lock?" To the surprise of Mikael and Marjatta there was a puzzled note in the voice of the unknown man. "I hadn't thought of that. I don't know. I can't see anything on this side. Is there a keyhole on your side?"

"No." Mikael was frowning as he said, "But *you* should know if there's a lock. Isn't this your yacht?"

There was a moment or so of silence, then the unseen man said very soberly, "Look—and I know this is going to sound very silly—I didn't even know until now that this boat was a yacht. I can hear the engine, but it could have been a fishing boat for all I knew. How big is it?"

"That's funny," Marjatta whispered to Mikael. "He should know where he is. Ask him who he is. Tell him the name of the yacht, then ask him his name."

"All right." Mikael raised his voice, "Sir, I think this yacht is called *Red Dolphin*. I suppose it's about ten or twelve meters long. The name is in Swedish. What's your name? And . . . er . . . why didn't you know what kind of a boat the *Red Dolphin* is?"

Again there was a long silence, followed by a strange apologetic laugh.

"You're going to find this hard to believe. I . . . er . . . I'm afraid I don't even *know* what my name is. I just can't remember who I am, or where I came from. I can't even remember how I got on this boat. I just woke up a while ago . . . and here I was. Who are you? You sound young. Oh, and where are we?"

Mikael and Marjatta exchanged puzzled, half-frightened glances. That a man should be aboard a magnificent yacht like the *Red Dolphin*, be imprisoned in the forward cabin, and know neither his own name, nor where the yacht was—or even that it was a yacht—seemed like a mouthful of lies.

"I'll try to open the door again," Mikael said, but Marjatta began answering the man's questions.

"I'm Marjatta Ekman, and my brother Mikael is with me. He's fourteen and I'm thirteen. We were rowing home with some boxes of Baltic herring, when we saw something in the porthole of this yacht—"

"A burning rag," Mikael added. "And we were coming across to find out if you needed help, but then the wind turned the yacht off course and she ran us down."

"Ran you down! Phew!" There was a whistle of dismay from the man in the forward cabin. "I heard the dog barking, and I thought I felt a bump, but I didn't realize what it was. Are you hurt?"

"We're wet," Mikael said gruffly, "and we lost our boat. Father won't be happy, that's for sure. He—"

"Mikael, the water," Marjatta interrupted. "It must be pouring in. We'd better do something."

Mikael looked down and saw that his sister was right. During the few minutes they had been in the cabin the water level had risen at least another inch. It was also spurting along one side of the sliding door from more than a foot up, suggesting that there was even more water in the forward cabin.

"If you could open the door," the unseen man suggested anxiously. "There's half a meter of water in here. We must be leaking very badly. Did we hit a rock when the ship lurched so badly? I thought we'd run aground."

"She slid along a rock," Mikael agreed. Then he added, "Look, sir, I think the best thing would be for us to head for the nearest island. I'll speed up the engine. Once she's beached we'll get help. This door just won't budge."

There was a moment of silence, then the unseen man pleaded, "You won't leave me, will you? This cabin is like a prison. I just can't get out of here. The portholes are too small for me to get through. I tried to break the door down, but all I did was bruise my shoulders. If you leave me, I don't know what will happen."

"The only way we can leave you, sir," Mikael pointed out grimly, "is by swimming. Our own boat was smashed. The yacht's dinghy broke loose, and we're at least a mile from the nearest island."

"You needn't worry, sir," Marjatta assured the prisoner. "My brother will speed up the engine, and I'll stay here. What's your dog's name?" She asked that question because the terrier was now reaching up and licking her hand.

"The dog! I have no idea what his name is. I don't even know what he looks like."

Marjatta shook her head at Mikael, who hurried down to the stern. After studying the engine controls for a moment or so, he gently pushed on the throttle lever. The engine responded at once. He pushed until the throttle lever was as far forward as it would go, and by that time the *thrum-thrum-thrum* of the diesel had changed to a deep-throated growl. Within seconds the yacht was quivering from stem to stern, plowing through the water at a speed which built up very quickly from about one knot an hour to nearly seven.

Suddenly there was a shout from the man in the cabin: "Hey, are you there? Stop the engine! The water's pouring in here, pouring in! I'll be drowned in minutes!"

The water was not rising so quickly in the main cabin, but Marjatta could see it spurting in along the sides of the door, proving that the unseen prisoner was telling the truth. The leak was in the bow, and the forward cabin was beginning to flood.

Mikael throttled back the engine, thinking that their speed must have been the cause of the sudden rush of water. With the yacht moving very slowly the water came in less quickly, but it was still coming in at a dangerous rate. The level in the main cabin was rising.

Mikael entered the main cabin to see for himself, then hurried out again with Marjatta at his heels. Both were thinking the same thing—how far away was the nearest island?

The sun was still shining. The afternoon remained

calm and peaceful. Sea birds were winging their way about, intent on finding food. It seemed impossible that so much had happened since the young Finns left their father and his fisherman friends less than two hours earlier.

The nearest island was quite far away. Which one it was they did not know—there were scores and scores of islands. Some were inhabited; some were not, because the low cliffs made landing by boat difficult.

"We'll head for that one," Mikael said. "I only hope it has a good beach."

"We could anchor," Marjatta pointed out, and Mikael laughed scornfully.

"Oh, yes, we could anchor," he mocked, "but what about that poor man in the cabin? If we don't get him out before the yacht sinks—well!" and he shrugged. Marjatta's eyes widened with sudden horror. Yes, they had to find a beach onto which they could run the *Red Dolphin*. Otherwise it would sink and drown the man imprisoned in the forward cabin.

Mikael cautiously opened up the engine throttle again. He did not give the diesel full power, but even so, there was a yell of anguish from the unseen prisoner. The water was rising rapidly once more.

Rummaging through the lockers as the yacht moved toward the island, Marjatta and Mikael found all kinds of things which were of no use to them. There were lovely woolen blankets in waterproof bags and oilskin suits far better than any their father had ever been able to afford. There were tins of paint, splendid new brushes, but no ax, which was what Mikael was looking for. With a good ax, or even a heavy hammer, he could break down the jammed sliding door.

It was Marjatta who found the pump. Mikael fitted it on deck and began swinging the long handle up and down. Within seconds water came gushing out.

"I'll pump, you steer," Mikael said. "I don't like this at all. The yacht has a lot of water in her."

He pumped like a madman. Marjatta steered the yacht on a course for the island, then went into the cabin to see what was happening. Despite the fact that her brother was pumping as fast as anyone could, the water level was still rising. It was now almost a foot deep in the main cabin, and it was gushing through the jammed door at the sides from a height of over three feet. The water was obviously coming in from near the bow and flooding straight into the forward cabin.

"What's happening?" the man yelled.

"Mikael is pumping water out, and we're heading for an island," Marjatta assured him. "Don't worry, we'll be there soon."

"I hope so. This place is going to be completely flooded in a matter of minutes." The man did not try to hide his anxiety as he added, "I just looked through the porthole. If we sink much lower, that'll be the end."

"Shut the portholes," Marjatta suggested. "If you do that—"

"I can't," the man cut in abruptly. "There's no glass in them. Something's happened, and almost every bit of glass has been smashed away. Please hurry, or I know I'm going to drown."

"I'll speed up the engine," Marjatta promised. Rushing back, she opened the throttle to its widest, so that once again the engine note was like muffled thunder.

Back at the tiller she could see that the island was much nearer. She could see there were low cliffs, topped by a mass of small trees. Probably dwarf juniper and pine—these were about the only trees which would grow on such wind-swept islands. But, straining her eyes, Marjatta could make out no sign of a beach. It seemed as if the cliffs ran straight down to the water.

Hurrying down to the cabin again to check on the water level, she found the fox terrier whimpering on top of the lockers.

"There's nothing to worry about," Marjatta told him, stroking his head. But as she spoke, the imprisoned man, hearing her voice, called to her.

"Is that you, Marjatta?"

"Yes."

"How long before we reach the shore?" the man asked anxiously. "Water is beginning to splash in through the portholes."

Marjatta almost said, "Are you sure?" but checked the words. The man would never say such a thing unless it were true.

"I'll head straight for the beach," she promised. "We'll get there, I promise." But as she hurried out, she had a feeling they might not make it. Once water began to flood through the portholes the end would be swift. The yacht's bow would sink lower, and—she shivered at the thought of what would follow. The forward cabin would

flood, and the man imprisoned there would not be able
to get out.

As she returned to the tiller her brother called, "Better steer along the coast a little, Marja. There doesn't
seem to be any real beach here. We can't risk—"

"We've *got* to risk landing. Now!" Marjatta's face was
pale in the afternoon sun. "We'll sink in a minute or two.
Water is coming in through those broken portholes."

"But . . ." Mikael was about to protest that if there was
no beach on which to drive the bow of the *Red Dolphin*,
the yacht would sink in deep water. In some of these
places where the cliffs ran right down to the sea, the
water at the foot of the cliffs was very deep indeed.

He renewed his pumping, perspiration streaming
down his face. Marjatta stood at the tiller, her eyes fixed
on the island. Then she felt something wet pressed
against the palm of her hand. The little fox terrier had
left the cabin. Water dripped off him. He was not whining now but simply looking at Marjatta and silently
pleading with her to help his master.

There was a lump in Marjatta's throat as she reached
down to press a comforting hand on the dog's head.
"We're doing everything we can," she whispered.
"Everything. Sit here, there's a good boy."

A minute later Mikael stopped pumping and rushed
around to his sister. He grabbed her, and they both
braced themselves for the shock as the *Red Dolphin*
swung ponderously around a savage-looking tooth of
rock and headed straight for the island.

Marooned

3

WITH ITS BILGES flooded and so much water in the cabins, the *Red Dolphin* hit the beach like an army tank. There was a crunching, grinding roar; the yacht shuddered and pebbles were thrown up in a great cloud as the bow drove into the steep sloping beach. The mast shook and the rigging flapped.

Even though Marjatta and Mikael had been prepared for the shock, they were sent sliding along the deck. The dog, yelping in terror, went rolling over and over. As the yacht lifted, a great mass of water swept from its flooded bow down toward the stern. It swamped the engine cockpit, then splashed overboard, carrying with it odds and ends from the cabins.

For about half a minute Mikael and Marjatta lay flat, too shaken and shocked to move. The yapping of the dog brought Mikael to his feet. The *Red Dolphin* was quivering and heeling slightly as it settled onto the pebbly beach.

Dragging his sister to her feet, Mikael pushed her to the side. "Jump . . . jump before she rolls over," he yelled.

As soon as Marjatta had jumped, Mikael followed. The

dog watched and whined pathetically, terrified at being left behind. When they were a dozen yards from the water's edge the youngsters stopped and looked back. The *Red Dolphin* had settled on an almost even keel. The dog, which had apparently run down into the cabin, reappeared, barking excitedly. When Mikael called to him he turned and dropped into the engine cockpit again, only to reappear a moment later, barking even more shrilly. He was not going to desert his master!

"The man!" Marjatta and Mikael exclaimed, remembering the prisoner in the forward cabin.

"You stay here," Mikael ordered.

Running down the beach, he climbed back onto the yacht. Marjatta's heart was thumping as she watched him drop down into the engine cockpit. Suppose the yacht swung onto her side? Suppose she slid back into deep water?

After a minute or so, straining to catch the least sound from the yacht, Marjatta too climbed aboard. She had a feeling that her brother needed her.

When she splashed down to the main cabin, where the luxurious carpet oozed water at each step, she found Mikael all too glad to see her. The sliding door dividing the forward and the main cabin, which had kept them from helping the imprisoned man, must have been shaken loose when the *Red Dolphin* rammed the beach. The water had rushed out, leaving the man lying face down on the cabin floor.

"Is he dead?" Marjatta gasped.

"I don't know, but we'd better get him out and onto the beach. We can't do anything for him here."

This was easier said than done. By the time they had dragged him up on deck, then lowered him to the beach, and finally pulled him beyond the reach of the waves, Marjatta and Mikael both were completely exhausted. They lay and panted while the little dog sniffed at all three in turn, and whimpered when the stranger refused to respond after having his face vigorously licked.

Finally the two youngsters sat up. "If it's safe to go back, Mikael, what about seeing if there are any blankets, and matches," Marjatta suggested. "I'll collect some driftwood for a fire."

Mikael nodded and went back to the *Red Dolphin*. Marjatta, after a quick look at the man they had rescued, began to gather firewood. She had a feeling she ought to be doing something for him, but she was afraid he was dead, and the thought sent an icy shiver down her back.

Her brother was less squeamish. When he came back with two bundles of cream-colored blankets, wrapped in cellophane, and completely dry, he said, "Marja, you go aboard and see if you can find something to make a hot drink—a pot, coffee or cocoa, sugar. And look for dry towels. I found these blankets in one of the lockers in the main cabin. If you find a towel, better dry yourself."

"And what about you?"

"I'll see if I can dry him." Mikael pointed to the silent figure. "If I give him a good rubbing with a blanket and then wrap him up, maybe he'll come round. He's not dead."

"Are you sure? How do you know?"

"I saw his hand twitch," Mikael said as he stooped to stroke the little dog which was pawing anxiously at him.

"It's okay," he said to the dog. "Your master's going to be all right in no time."

Marjatta went to board the yacht, and Mikael stripped off his clothes and gave himself a vigorous toweling with one of the blankets. He spread his wet clothes out on the pebble beach and wrapped himself in another blanket. Then he stripped the wet clothes off the unconscious man. He rubbed and pummeled the limp figure until the white skin glowed pink, but there was no response.

Panting from his exertions, Mikael finally sat back on his heels. "Had a nasty bang on the head," he murmured, frowning at the swollen forehead and the bruise, already turning an ugly blue-black. "Still, he's alive. His heart's beating."

When Marjatta finally returned from the yacht she carried an aluminum kettle, cups, a tin containing two unopened packets of biscuits, sugar, coffee, cocoa, and a packet holding eleven boxes of safety matches.

Mikael looked at her and gasped. Like him, she was clad in a blanket, but she had cut a hole in the middle of it through which she had poked her head. Slits in the material served as armholes, and a piece of cord fastened the garment at the waist. "Do the same with your blanket," she urged Mikael.

For the next hour and a half they scarcely stopped working. After they had drunk the cocoa Marjatta made they started to make themselves comfortable. The fire was built up, but since they had three lots of wet clothing, Mikael decided to rig up a line on which it could be hung.

He found a long length of rope aboard the *Red Dol-phin*. Tying one end to the mast, he carried the other ashore and fastened it to a rock at the foot of the low cliffs. Then all the wet clothes were strung up to dry.

Marjatta did what she could to bring the rescued man back to consciousness. She bathed his forehead in sea water and massaged his hands. All the time the little dog watched anxiously, whining and occasionally looking up at her as if asking how his master was progressing.

It was the dog who first discovered that the man had regained consciousness. The children had gone back to the yacht's cabin to try to find some food more substantial than biscuits when the dog began to bark. Within seconds Mikael and Marjatta were kneeling by the side of the man, whose eyes were now open.

"What happened? Where am I? Who are you?" he mumbled, while the terrier barked and barked, his tail wagging furiously.

"Drink this first," Mikael suggested, hurriedly filling a cup with cocoa.

"Thank you!" Frowning, the man slowly sat up and began to drink the steaming cocoa. Finally, to their amazement, he asked, "Tell me . . . do you know who I am?"

"You asked that before," Mikael said, puzzled. "You *must* know where you came from. Anyway, don't you recognize your dog?"

"Is . . . is that *my* dog?"

"I'm sure he is, sir," Marjatta said eagerly. "He's been so anxious about you, I don't think there's any doubt that he's yours."

The man put his hand on his forehead and closed his eyes.

"Lie down and sleep," Mikael suggested. "You'll probably remember everything tomorrow."

The man nodded and lay down, but after a few moments he struggled to a sitting position again. "My clothes—where are they? There must be something in my clothes that says who I am. Weren't there any papers in my pockets?"

Mikael brought the trousers and the very fine seaman's jersey the man had been wearing when they brought him ashore. There was some Swedish money in the trouser pockets, an expensive cigarette lighter, a pocket-knife, and a handkerchief.

Going aboard the *Red Dolphin* again, Mikael found a jacket lying on the floor. But the wallet and notebook he took from the pockets were so wet that the money and the leaves of the notebook were stuck together.

"We'll put them on a flat stone by the fire," Mikael said. "They'll dry out by morning and then I'm sure you'll be able to read them."

Nodding wearily, the stranger lay down. They covered him with an extra blanket, and very soon he was fast asleep.

By now the day was ending. The sun had disappeared somewhere beyond the mountains of unseen Sweden. The sea was settling down to a calmness which made it look like a huge lake. Sea birds were beginning to settle for the night; they looked like specks of paper resting on a dull mirror. The cliffs behind the spot where Mikael had lighted their fire were now bathed in darkness, darkness relieved only by the glow from the burning driftwood.

"Do you think one of us should stay awake?" Marjatta asked.

"What for? There's no one going to come here during the night. What are you afraid of—savages?" Mikael laughed.

"Of course not," Marjatta said. "I was just wondering —suppose he wakes up during the night and wants something. Or suppose the yacht begins to move. It could slip back into deep water, couldn't it?"

"If he woke up, we would hear him," Mikael pointed out. "And as for the yacht—if you will look, my dear, worried sister, you will see that I lugged the anchor ashore and dug it deep into the beach."

"Oh, you're always so cocky!" Marjatta was annoyed. "I was only trying to think of anything which could go wrong."

"I know." Mikael grinned. "And I was only pulling your leg. But if the yacht did slip off into deep water, we couldn't do anything. Some of her planking is smashed in, so she'd sink. I think we should both go to sleep. In the morning we'll see if we can repair the damage—or signal for help."

"I think we should catch some fish," Marjatta said, trying to hide a yawn. "I'm hungry. I suppose we'd better not open the second packet of biscuits—still, I'm sure we can catch some fish for breakfast. Should we have another biscuit?"

"Have some more cocoa," Mikael suggested. "You know, Marja, I was just thinking. It's funny, really, but no one will be worrying the least bit about us. Mother will think that we've stayed with Dad, so she won't worry. Dad will be certain that we're at home, so he won't worry, either. Won't they be amazed when they find out what happened?"

They decided not to keep the fire burning through the night. Mikael put some dry wood aboard the yacht in case it rained before morning. They had plenty of matches, so lighting the fire again would present no problem. They finished off what was left of the cocoa, then scooped out little hollows in the pebbles for their hips, and snuggled down.

The moon, not quite full, came silently into view. It transformed the wall of low cliffs behind them into a mysterious pattern of gray and black. And where water trickling from the rocks caught the moonlight and reflected its white brilliance, there were glittering streams of silver.

The night was quiet. The soft lapping of small waves on the beach, and around the hull of the *Red Dolphin*, was like a lullaby. The dog curled up against Mikael's feet and fell asleep instantly. Mikael lay on his back and began picking out the various stars he knew. Marjatta's thoughts turned to home as she wondered what her mother would be doing.

A few minutes later the fire, already burning low, caved in. A few sparks drifted upward. The dog, startled even in his sleep by the slight sound, opened one eye, then closed it again. Mikael and Marjatta, fast asleep, never moved.

As the night went by, the moon rode silently across the heavens. Dropping downward in the west it was finally hidden behind a bank of cloud. A gray line appeared on the eastern horizon. A few minutes later a flight of eider ducks passed along the coast with a faint winnowing of wings.

The terrier heard them, and one ear lifted, but drooped again as the ducks sped on their way. As the light in the east grew rapidly brighter two red-billed oyster catchers came by. They circled the stranded yacht and shattered the quiet with their shrill piping calls.

The dog was on his feet in an instant, and his warning bark shook the sleep from the eyes of both Mikael and Marjatta. For a moment or so they lay still, then as if both realized they had spent the night in a strange place, they rose, yawning and rubbing the sleep from their eyes.

The dog came over, whining softly, and tugged at the fringe of Mikael's blanket. His action reminded them of the unknown yachtsman, and they turned to look at him.

"He hasn't moved," Marjatta whispered. "You don't think he's—"

"No!" Mikael said sharply, though the same frightening thought had occurred to him. "If *you* were knocked on the head like—"

He was interrupted by Marjatta. "Have you moved them?" she asked. She was staring at the flat stone on which they had laid the wallet and the notebook.

"Moved what? Oh, the wallet and the notebook!" Mikael looked around as if half expecting to see the missing articles somewhere close by. Shaking his head, he muttered emphatically, "I didn't move them. Why should I?"

"We didn't put them back in . . ." Marjatta began, then stopped, her eyes goggling. Too amazed to speak, she lifted a hand to point. Mikael looked, but could see nothing out of the ordinary. Then Marjatta found her tongue. "The clothes!" she gasped. "The clothes you hung on the line! Where are they?"

Mikael looked toward the cliff behind them. He had tied one end of the clothes rope to a boulder at the foot of the cliff. The boulder was still there, but there was no sign of a rope, or even a fragment of rope.

He looked eastward along the beach, for the wind invariably came from the west. If the clothes had been blown away they would be scattered on the beach to the east.

There was nothing. The beach looked exactly as it had looked the previous evening—pebbles, some seaweed, a few large pieces of driftwood, but no clothing.

"Someone has been here," Marjatta said, and she could not keep the anxiety from her voice.

"Don't be silly! Who could have been here?" Mikael asked. "Probably a wind came up in the night, and—"

"It's you who are talking silly," Marjatta interrupted, her voice becoming shrill with worry. "If there had been a wind it would have wakened us. And could a wind have blown the wallet away?"

Mikael had no answer to that. And there was a queer little cold feeling in his stomach, for he had just seen something which his sister had not yet noticed—a piece of rope hanging down the *Red Dolphin*'s mast. It was what was left of the rope he had tied there the night before, and his needle-sharp eyes could see that the rope had been cut.

Trying to comfort Marjatta he said, "I'll just walk down the beach, and if I don't find our clothes—"

"No, don't!" Marjatta exclaimed. "I'm telling you, someone's been here while we were asleep."

"Well, I'll have a look at the yacht," he insisted.

Mikael went aboard the *Red Dolphin*. A quick glance at the piece of rope proved that he was right—it had been cut by a sharp knife. In the cabin nothing seemed wrong. If anything had been taken he did not know what it was.

"What are we going to do?" Marjatta asked when he rejoined her on the beach. "I'm frightened, Mikael."

"There isn't anything to be frightened of," Mikael said, trying to reassure her. "I expect some passing fisherman saw the yacht on the beach and came to see if—"

"Are our people thieves, Mikael?" Marjatta asked quietly. "Would a passing fisherman steal from sleeping people? You know they wouldn't."

Mikael nodded. What his sister said was true enough. Had any of the Finns who fished from the islands come ashore they would have realized there was something wrong with the *Red Dolphin,* and they would have stayed to help, not to steal from the sleepers.

The little dog soon reminded them of another problem. He pawed at Mikael, whining, then nosed at the tin containing the solitary packet of biscuits. It was his way of telling them that he was hungry.

"I'm hungry, too," Mikael said. Opening the packet, he tossed two biscuits to the dog. He gave his sister two, and took two for himself. Then he folded the paper over the remaining biscuits and laid the package in the tin.

"You light the fire, Marjatta," he suggested, "and make some cocoa. I'll see if I can catch some fish. I saw some fishing lines in the cabin when I was getting the blankets."

"Don't go far away," Marjatta insisted. She called the dog to her as Mikael turned to board the *Red Dolphin* again. Picking the largest embers from the fire, she began to split them with her knife. Whittled into thin slivers, the wood soon caught fire. Within five minutes she was adding more wood to the growing blaze.

Mikael got one of the fishing lines out of the cabin and baited the hooks with part of a dead starfish he picked up earlier at the water's edge. He was not very optimistic about catching anything, for the sea was a dead calm. He knew their chances of a fish breakfast would have been better if there had been even a slight breeze to ruffle the water.

In the quiet of the morning he heard the *wee-wee-wee-wee* of wings even before a flight of redshanks came into view. Their brilliant red legs showing in the early morning sunshine, the birds came down at the water's edge and began seeking their breakfast in the shallows some forty yards farther down the beach. They were too busy to notice the whirr of the line when Mikael swung his hooks out, but when Marjatta called to ask how the fishing was going, they took fright and flew off.

"We'll have to make do with biscuits," Mikael said soberly as he jumped off the yacht and strode over to the fire. "How many biscuits are there left?"

"Only a few. I gave some more to the dog," Marjatta admitted. "He seemed so hungry."

"He's not as hungry as I am," Mikael growled, sitting down and sniffing at the steaming cocoa.

Marjatta poured a cup for him. As she was pouring

one for herself the yachtsman opened his eyes and struggled to a sitting position. His face was creased into a frown as if he were thinking hard.

The moment he moved, the dog flung himself across the man, yapping excitedly and pawing at him, his tail wagging furiously. Ignoring the dog, the man said, "I see you're still wearing the blankets. Are your clothes still wet?"

Marjatta shot a swift glance at her brother. Mikael scratched at his tousled hair for a moment, then admitted, "It looks like we haven't got any clothes. Someone must have come here during the night, because everything's gone—even the clothesline."

"Have they taken mine too?" the man asked, startled.

"Yes," Mikael said. To Marjatta he added, "Pour a third mug, Marja."

"Do we have any food?" the man asked. "I'm desperately hungry."

Again Marjatta looked quickly at Mikael. Then, holding out the almost empty biscuit tin, she said, "I'm afraid we only have these biscuits, sir. We'll try and get something else. We were thinking of exploring the island. There's sure to be someone living here, and . . ." There she paused, for the yachtsman had gently pushed the tin away.

"I've just discovered that I'm not hungry," he said. For a moment there was the hint of a twinkle in his eyes. "At least, shall I say that you're much hungrier than I am. No, no, I refuse to have anything but a drink," he insisted as Marjatta pushed the biscuit tin toward him again.

"You must have something, sir," Mikael said. "You only had one biscuit last night, and—"

"You eat them," the yachtsman said. "You're going to look for help, and I can't think of anything worse than being hungry when you're young." He took the mug of cocoa Mikael had poured for him, and began to sip.

He asked them where they were, but there were so many islands dotting these waters that neither Mikael nor Marjatta knew the name of this one. Nor did they know for sure whether anyone lived here. Some islands had a family or two living on them; some had a small village; others were uninhabited.

Mikael gave the last biscuit to the dog, who gulped it down, then licked at a crumb that had fallen among the stones.

"If anybody sees you they'll think the druids have come back to earth," the yachtsman said, smiling. "And I suppose if I had the strength to stand up I'd look as strange. A cream-colored blanket, eh? Well, well, well!"

"Who were the druids, sir?" Marjatta asked, somehow feeling much happier now that the strange yachtsman seemed in a brighter mood.

"Oh, they lived in England hundreds of years ago," the yachtsman explained. "I imagine they probably dressed much as you are dressed now, except that their woolen garments would not be as soft or as clean as the ones you're wearing. Anyway, I suggest you walk around the island. Look for smoke. People can hide a house, but if they have a fire you should see the smoke. The air is so still, smoke will just rise straight up."

"Could we take the dog, sir?" Mikael asked, adding a

little shamefacedly, "in case we meet the man who stole our clothes."

"Take him. I'm not sure he's my dog, anyway." And as an afterthought, since the dog was huddling up to him and whining softly, "Better get some rope and put a loop around his neck. He may not want to come with you."

Prisoners

4

FIVE MINUTES LATER Mikael and Marjatta and the dog started off. Not far from their little camp they came to a place where a deep gully in the cliff face enabled them to climb up off the beach. One or two small bushes grew in the gully, and there were several patches of cloudberries. The fruit was almost ripe, and Marjatta began to pick them and pop them into her mouth.

"I could eat a bucketful," she murmured, but Mikael was impatient to get on.

"If we don't find anybody we can pick cloudberries on our way back," he said. "I'd rather have a plate of fish than two buckets of cloudberries. Come on."

They scrambled up the last dozen feet of the gully, the dog coming along only because of the rope about his neck. As they came out on top of the cliffs, to a landscape dotted with dwarf pines and junipers, a man stepped from behind a clump of pines. He was a typical island fisherman, looking shorter than he was because of his powerful shoulders and the heavy lumberjacket he wore. His chin was dark and unshaven, which was nothing out of the ordinary. What neither Mikael nor Marjatta liked,

however, was the scowling face, and the shotgun he pointed at them.

"This saves me the trouble of coming down for you," he said. Then, with a jerk of the shotgun, he added, "Come on, I want you over at my place, where I can keep an eye on you and where you can't do any harm."

"Harm!" Mikael said, half frightened, half angry. "What do you mean? Who could we harm? If you'll come back we'll show you the yacht we were on when she ran aground."

"I saw you run aground," the man said sourly. "Here, keep that dog down or . . . That's better," he added as Mikael shortened the rope holding the dog. The anger in Mikael's voice had made the dog growl and strain at the rope.

"Yes," the man repeated, "I saw you run aground, and during the night I came back and took your clothes. I must say you look quite a sight in blankets. Quick, now, I'm in a hurry." He moved behind the children and poked Mikael in the back with the muzzle of his shotgun. "Get moving. You too," he growled to Marjatta.

The island was about half a mile across. Like many of the islands which lie off the southwest coast of Finland, it was rocky, with soil so thin that it would have been impossible for a farmer to plow the land.

Marjatta looked regretfully at the patches of cloudberries and crowberries growing in abundance. It told her one thing which frightened her—no women lived on this island. Had there been even one woman she would have been gathering the fruit to make jam for the winter months.

The quietness was broken by an excited yelp from the dog and a shriek of alarm from Marjatta. An adder, bathing on a flat stone, had suddenly uncoiled itself. With its forked tongue darting in and out, its eyes shining like jewels, the snake lunged at Marjatta's bare ankles.

From earliest days the island children were taught to keep a careful watch for adders when they went out to gather berries or play away from the home clearing.

Even though adders were hunted mercilessly on the
islands where fisher families lived, the reptiles were still
a danger. The bite of an adder meant death unless help
came quickly.

Marjatta tried to leap away as the adder uncoiled and
moved to strike at her. Just in time the little terrier got
between them and snapped at the diamond-shaped head.
Missing his aim, his sharp teeth closed on thin air. Yet
he did succeed in throwing the adder to one side.

This gave Marjatta her chance. Mikael grabbed his
sister and dragged her out of range. But the dog was
not so lucky.

Instead of retreating he sprang again, barking furiously. The adder uncoiled itself a second time and
struck with frightening speed. Its fangs took the terrier
in the cheek, and the few seconds the adder held on
were long enough for the deadly poison to be pumped
down its hollow teeth into the wound.

With a sideways flick of his head the terrier dislodged
the adder, throwing it a yard away. Mikael and Marjatta
watched in wide-eyed shock. The dog pounced on the
snake before it had time to recover and shook it so
savagely that it died without being able to strike again.

Suddenly the man with the gun spoke angrily. "You
should always watch for snakes. You're darn lucky you
aren't—hey, come here—" Mikael had rushed over to the
dog and was dragging him away from the dead adder.

He stooped and turned the dog's head to see where
the snake had bitten him. But the man grabbed him by
the shoulder. "Come on, I don't have time to waste," he

said, trying to pull Mikael to his feet. "If the dog's been bitten—"

"He was—in the cheek," Mikael said, already fumbling for the knife he had pushed into his rope belt. "I'm going to—"

"You're not going to do anything," the man answered gruffly. "If he's been bitten he's as good as dead!"

Mikael jumped up and twisted out of the man's grasp. Gasping with anger and indignation, he said, "I'm going to do whatever I can for the dog. Marjatta would have been bitten if it wasn't for—*ouch!*"

The man had suddenly thrust the muzzle of his gun into Mikael's ribs. "That's your own fault, I didn't mean to hurt you," the man growled. "But when I say I don't have time to bother with the dog, I mean it. Come on."

"I'm not moving." The color was drained from Mikael's cheeks and his words came jerkily, but he faced the man defiantly. Tossing his sheathed knife to Marjatta he said, "See what you can do for him, Marja."

Marjatta caught the knife. Drawing the dog to her, she knelt down, cuddling his head in her lap.

The man tried to grab Mikael again, but he dodged away.

"Touch me or my sister and you won't get me *near* your house. I'll run back to the yacht," he said. "Now, just try and stop her."

The man swiftly changed his grip on the gun, grabbing it by the barrel and swinging it like an ax. Mikael dodged, then picked up a stone. It was about the size of a tennis ball. He drew back his arm and waited, and the man with the gun hesitated. At such short range the boy could hardly miss, and a stone like that could hurt. It could even knock a man out.

Slowly the man swung his gun around until his hand was over the trigger guard and the muzzle was pointing at Mikael. His eyes were blazing with anger, yet for some reason he did not do anything—just stood and stared.

Meanwhile Marjatta was doing what she could for the fox terrier. From the time when they were small their father and mother had warned them about adders and taught them what to do if an adder bit them. It was painful but simple: make a cross-shaped cut over the bite, then suck hard at the wound to draw the poison out.

Marjatta did this. Holding the fox terrier tightly, she managed to make a tiny little cut over the pinpoint wounds where the adder had bitten the cheek. Then she put her lips to the cut and sucked. It was not a pleasant thing to do, but she would have done more—the little dog had probably saved her life.

"Come on, come on," the man growled. "If you haven't saved him by now you never will."

"What can we do now?" Marjatta asked, ignoring the man and turning to her brother. "I don't know if I've got all the poison out, and—"

Bang! Marjatta jumped in terror. The man had deliberately fired his gun at the ground, where the leaden shot threw up a puff of brown dust.

At the thunderbolt roar of the gun the little terrier

leaped from Marjatta's arms. Yelping, he raced back the way he had come, disappearing among the stunted trees. Finally his terrified yelps died away.

"Now no more fooling," the man snarled as he hastily ejected the spent cartridge and pushed another in its place, so that the gun was ready to be fired again. "I have no time to waste. Get moving." With a curt nod he indicated the direction in which they were to go.

Marjatta stared at him, an expression of disgust on her face. "I hope you are not a Finn," she said coldly. "I'd be ashamed to think any Finn would be so cruel. You are worse than that." She pointed to the dead snake.

"Come on," Mikael said quietly. As he spoke he was pushing the stone inside his blanket robe, but the man had seen it, and with a vicious jab from his gun muzzle he knocked it to the ground.

A few minutes later the three of them came through the last of the pines and junipers and looked down a shrub-dotted slope to the sea. Away in the distance were more islands, and beyond them the mainland of Finland itself.

Not far from the beach were three buildings. One was a single-story house. A thin curl of blue smoke was rising from its stone chimney. The next building had an open end and was obviously a boathouse and storage place for nets. The third building was even smaller. It had barred windows and a door. The windows had no glass so that air could circulate about the dried fish which was kept there. The thin iron bars were to keep robber sea birds from raiding the fish storage during hard weather.

An old, gray-bearded man sat on a bench in front of the house. His gnarled fingers were busy with shuttle and cord, repairing nets. He did not look up until the man with the gun yelled, "I got them!" To Mikael and Marjatta he said, "In there you go," and he pointed to the fish shed with the barred windows.

"I am not going in there," Mikael said stubbornly, but he hesitated when the man suddenly grabbed Marjatta and pushed her into the shed, slamming the door and quickly swinging the bar which fastened it in place.

Laying his gun against the door, the man threw off his coat and began to roll up the sleeves of his coarse shirt. "Are you going to go in, or do I have to put you in? If I have to put you in, you'll be sorry."

Mikael looked at the bulging muscles on the man's forearms. He could see that, like most of the men from the islands, whose constant rowing and hauling on dripping, herring-filled nets gave them tremendous strength in the arms and shoulders, this man would be very strong indeed. Mikael was strong for his age, but he was only fourteen. In a fight with the man he would lose very quickly.

"I'd go in if I was you, boy," advised the old man, laying aside the nets he had been mending. "You won't gain anything by being hurt—and Timo is at his best when he's fighting someone smaller than himself."

"Shut up, you old fool," Timo snarled, as he finished rolling up his sleeves. He turned to Mikael, "Well, do you go in or do I put you in?"

"Go in, boy, go in," the old man urged.

Mikael turned, lifted the door bolt, and joined his sister in the shed.

"He's horrible," Marjatta said, sobbing. "I'm sure he would have killed you."

"No, I wouldn't." Timo was closing the door, and there was a grin on his dark unshaven face as he added, "I just would have walloped you. Same as I'll do to your father if he tries to get away."

"My father?" Mikael and Marjatta spoke together, and Mikael added, "He's not here!"

Now it was Timo's turn to look puzzled. Picking up the shotgun again, he came to the front barred window. "What do you mean, 'he's not here'? Isn't the fellow with the red yacht your father?"

"Of course he isn't," Marjatta said scornfully. "We don't even know him."

"Don't lie to me," Timo said angrily. "If you don't know who he is, how come you're with him in the yacht, eh? Tell me that—and don't lie. I can tell when little children lie," he added sarcastically.

"You're very clever, aren't you?" Marjatta taunted.

But she shrank back when Timo pressed his face against the bars of the window and roared, "Give me more back talk and I'll put you across my knees, young lady. I know what's good for youngsters like you. Now . . . talk," and he glared at Mikael.

"Can't we have something to eat first?" Mikael asked. "We didn't have anything last night except some biscuits. We're starving."

"After you've talked," Timo snarled.

In as few words as possible Mikael told him how they
had first noticed the yacht, heard the dog barking, seen
the smoking rag thrust through a broken porthole, and
gone aboard to see if the yachtsman on the *Red Dolphin*
needed help.

Timo listened in silence. When Mikael ended his story
he asked, "Is the fellow badly hurt?"

Mikael shrugged, then explained, "He was unconscious when we got him off the yacht, but he's all right
now. I mean he's conscious, though he hasn't stood up
yet, and he doesn't seem to know who he is."

"All right. Stay where you are," he ordered. "Dad," he
added to the old man, "you see that they don't get out,
or you'll get something you won't like." Then he turned
away.

"What about something to eat?" Mikael called.

"You can wait," Timo yelled over his shoulder. "An
hour or so won't kill you. I've been hungry often enough,
so I should know."

With that he stalked away, and neither of the prisoners could see where he was going. The old man, busily
stuffing tobacco into an old pipe, came over to make
sure that the bar was safely across the door. After that he
stood staring down toward the sea, apparently watching
his son walk down to the beach.

"Listen, sir, what's going on? Why are we locked in
here?" Mikael knew it was no use being angry with the
old man. Maybe if he talked quietly to him he might
let them out.

The old man did not even look at him. He finished

filling his pipe, then struck a match. Staring toward the beach, he puffed at his pipe for several minutes before he turned and looked at Mikael and Marjatta's faces framed in the barred window. Then, plucking at his straggly gray beard, he shook his head and muttered in a disgusted voice, "Money! He'll do any mortal thing for money, so he will. If you offered him enough money he'd try and jump over the moon."

"What money will he get for keeping us here?" Marjatta asked. "We have no money. Our father is Juhan Ekman from Aalmo Island. Do you know him? Most old fishermen do."

"Juhan Ekman," the old man muttered, combing his fingers through his beard. "I knew a Juhan Ekman when I was a boy, but you couldn't be his children. I'm eighty-four. Juhan Ekman was about my age."

"Our grandfather!" Mikael said excitedly. Hoping to win the old man's sympathy, he added, "Imagine your knowing our grandfather! But he's dead now."

"He never was very strong," the old man muttered. "I always said he would die young."

"He was eighty-five when he died," Marjatta said half angrily. "And he wasn't weak. If he was weak . . ." and there she stopped, for Mikael had dug his elbow into her ribs.

"Don't start arguing with him," he whispered. "I'm trying to get him on our side." To the old man he said coaxingly, "You don't look eighty-four, sir. Most people don't mend nets anymore at your age!" But the old man did not look impressed. So Mikael went on, "You said your son would do anything for money. How will he get money by keeping us prisoners? The police will put him in jail when they find out."

"That's where you're wrong," the old man chuckled, striking another match to relight his pipe. "He'll take you to the police, along with the *Red Dolphin*, and the man who stole her."

"Stole her!" Mikael and Marjatta whispered the word

together and exchanged quick glances of bewilderment. Mikael tried to get more information from the old man. "How did you know the yacht was named the *Red Dolphin*?" Mikael asked. "You haven't seen her, have you?"

"Don't need to see her," the old man chuckled, wagging his head knowingly. "I knew all about the *Red Dolphin* as soon as my son-in-law Timo did. He's got a little radio, you see. Got it so he'd know what the weather's going to be like. Waste of good money, I told him. When I used to go fishing I looked at the sky, or at the sunset. You can tell by the feel of the wind if the weather is going to change." He relit his pipe and sat down on a bench in front of the shed, puffing out clouds of smoke.

"Ask him about the yacht," Marjatta whispered, but there was no need for Mikael to say anything. The old man must have possessed very sharp ears, for he stood up and said, "The yacht! Maybe you think I don't know. Well, I'll tell you, just to prove that we know everything that goes on. You stole the red yacht from Mariehamn harbor."

"That's the main port in the Aland Islands," Marjatta said promptly. "We've been there with my father."

"Of course you have," the old man chuckled. "You went there to steal the yacht. She was at anchor waiting to be provisioned for her owner. Night before last she was there. But when morning came and the provision man arrived, the yacht was gone. The crew stayed the night on shore, and when they went to get her ready for the owner, there was no yacht."

"But *we* didn't steal her," Mikael insisted.

"And I'll tell you something else," the old man continued, wagging the stem of his pipe at his listeners. "There's a reward of five thousand Swedish crowns for anyone who finds her—and brings her back. That's where Timo comes in." The old man paused, nodding his head. "I sat in the house with him when the broadcast came through. I'll tell you he was plenty excited when he actually saw you run the yacht ashore. yesterday. He could see there was something wrong with her. She was low in the water. You must have run aground somewhere."

"We struck a reef," Mikael admitted rather sulkily. "But it wasn't our fault. We were—"

"It's never the fault of the man who's steering," the old man chuckled. "He always has some excuse. Anyway, Timo knew what to do. He says the yacht is damaged, and can't sail until she's been repaired."

"Then why did he take our clothes?" Marjatta demanded angrily.

"Just to make sure," was the calm reply, and the old man chuckled again. "Timo is clever. He's gone now for some friends. They'll help him take the yacht back to the Mariehamn police. They'll put your father in prison, so they will, and maybe you as well. You shouldn't steal, you know. It's very wrong."

Mikael heard his sister draw in a swift, deep breath and knew she was about to deny that they had stolen the yacht. He put a hand across her mouth and spoke quietly to the old man. "There's one thing you could do for us, sir. The little dog we had was bitten by an adder.

Please let us out so that we can find him. *He* didn't steal anything—and we don't want him to die."

"We'll only be away half an hour," Marjatta added to her brother's plea. "We'll come back, we promise."

"Bit by an adder, was it?" The old man shook his head. " 'Taint no use worrying about the dog if an adder bit him. He'll die, sure enough." Turning, he walked toward the house, leaving Marjatta with tears in her eyes.

An Accident

5

THE BLACK-AND-WHITE FOX TERRIER had not stopped running until he was back on the beach. The battle with the adder and the unexpected report of Timo's shotgun had so terrified him that his tail was still between his legs when he reached the camp. The yachtsman was sitting by the fire, gently rubbing the side of his head where the lump was beginning to go down a little.

"So you're back," he said, fondling the dog. "Where are the two kids? Broke away from them, huh?"

The dog lay against him for a minute or more, trembling violently. As his trembling died down, he whined, licked the yachtsman's arm, then drew away from him. He walked two or three yards along the beach, stopped, looked at the man, then whined again—a pleading whine. When the man did not move the dog came back, took a mouthful of the blanket and began to tug at it.

"I need this," the man said, laughing softly. "It happens to be the only clothing I have." Picking up a pebble, he tossed it into the sea. "Go on, boy, fetch it!"

The dog only looked at him and whined.

"You're a strange one," the yachtsman said, frowning.

"I don't know what you'd say if you could talk, but your
eyes are begging me to do something. What am I supposed to do, boy? Come and tell me. Come on, now," he
coaxed, holding out a hand.

The dog came back slowly, took the outstretched
fingers gently between his teeth, and then drew back.

"So you want me to follow you, eh?" The yachtsman
rose painfully to his feet. "All right, all right, but not so
fast. I'll have to get myself a rope or something to hold
this blanket on." As he tied a piece of cord around his
waist he murmured, "I must make an odd picture in this
rig. Hm!"

He frowned as he walked. Not only was he sore but
every muscle was stiff as a board. The dog trotted ahead
of him, stopping every few steps to look back. With ears
pricked and a comical expression of surprise on his face,
he seemed to be asking why the man was so slow.

They got to the cleft in the cliff face, the place where
it was possible to scramble up from the beach. The sun
was warm now, and bees were droning through the
heather which grew like a close-cut carpet between the
dwarf trees.

The dog trotted on ahead, but by the time they had
covered half the distance across the island it was ap-
parent there was something wrong with him. His slim
legs did not take him along so surely, and twice he staggered and seemed about to fall. He was beginning to feel
the effects of the adder's poison. Even though Marjatta
had sucked out much of the venom, some still remained.

They were about two hundred yards from the shed

and the other buildings when the fox terrier's legs refused to take him any further. He flopped onto his side, made a brave effort to get to his feet again, only to fall once more. He lay looking up as the man drew near. His dark eyes were pleading, and he whined softly.

"What's the matter, boy?" the man asked, kneeling down and taking the dog in his arms. "Are you ill? You can't be weak from starvation, can you? I saw the girl giving you biscuits last night, and . . . oh-ho, what's this?" Stroking the dog's head, he noticed for the first time the punctures made by the adder's fangs and the little cut Marjatta had made to help her suck out the venom. But never having seen a snake bite he had no idea what the punctures and the cut cheek meant.

Despite his own pain he rose and hurried on, carrying the dog. There was no doubt that this was a highly intelligent dog, who was trying to lead him somewhere. He was worried—not only for the animal but for fear some accident had befallen the children. Maybe they had sent the dog back for help.

Three minutes later he came to the top of the slope leading to the sea and the beach on the east side of the island. He could see one single sail. It was Timo's boat, on its way to another island.

For a moment or so the yachtsman, hugging the whimpering fox terrier closely, stared across the sunlit sea. Then, with a resigned shrug he muttered, "No use shouting to him. He's at least a mile away. Anyway, there must be someone in the house, I can see smoke coming from the chimney." To the dog he said, "Don't worry, little fellow, we'll do something for you soon," and he walked a little faster down the slope.

He was about thirty yards from the house when the old man came out. He was carrying a jug of coffee and

two enamel mugs in one hand and his son-in-law's shotgun in the other. At the sight of the approaching man,
clad as Mikael and Marjatta were in a cream-colored
blanket, the old man gasped, then hurriedly put the jug
of coffee and the mugs down on the ground. Cocking his
shotgun and shuffling forward, he yelled excitedly,
"What do you want here? Be off with you, or I'll put a
load of shot in your legs."

Hearing this, Mikael and Marjatta looked at one another, then both scrambled for a place at the window.
At sight of the yachtsman, staring in amazement at the
old man, Marjatta screamed for help. At her scream the
yachtsman almost let the little dog fall he was so sur-
prised, and the old man turned nervously toward the
shed.

"Let us out, sir," Mikael yelled, shaking the thin iron
bars in his excitement. "They locked us up, and we
didn't do anything wrong, anything!"

"You two get away from that window," the old man
threatened, shaking the gun menacingly. "Go on . . . get
away or I'll pepper you both."

Marjatta drew back a little, but Mikael stood his
ground. Marjatta tried to pull him away from the window. "He might shoot, Mikael."

"He won't dare!" Mikael said doggedly.

"What's going on?" The question came from the
yachtsman, who had quietly walked a dozen paces
nearer while the old man was threatening Marjatta and
Mikael.

At the question the old man started and turned. "You

get away from here!" he screamed, almost dancing with
rage. "I'm warning you . . . and I don't say things I don't
mean. Go on. Off with you!"

"Listen, old man," the yachtsman said quietly. "You're
going to get yourself into a lot of trouble if you wave
that gun about much more. If it goes off . . . and someone
is hurt—"

"You'll *all* get hurt if you don't do as I say," the old
man roared. Swinging round again, he pointed the gun
at the shed and yelled, "You get away from that window
or . . ."

At that moment, forgetting his stiff and aching muscles, the yachtsman tried to rush him. He tightened his
grip on the little dog who yelped in protest.

The startled old man turned quickly, and suddenly
there was the thunderous report of a gunshot and a
crash, as the charge of shot struck the planking of the
shed. An instant later Marjatta screamed.

Mikael had leaped to one side as the gun belched shot,
flame, and smoke. At his sister's scream he turned—just
in time to catch her as she fell. Her face was deathly pale
and she clutched her right leg.

Shocked, frightened, and almost too angry to know
what he was saying, Mikael yelled, "You old bully,
you've shot my sister! If you've killed her . . ." He could
not finish the sentence, for he was struggling to lower
Marjatta to the floor as gently as he could.

The moment she was on the ground he sprang to the
window again, hands grasping the thin, rusty bars. More
angry words were on his tongue, but none of them were

spoken, for the old man looked as if he, too, were going to collapse. All the color had drained from his weather-beaten face. The still-smoking shotgun had slipped from his shaking hands and his eyes were filled with horror and fear. His mouth was opening and closing as if he were trying to say something. But no sound came.

The yachtsman, pausing only long enough to set the little dog on the ground, hobbled swiftly to the shed. The old man followed him, now whimpering, "I didn't mean to do it. I didn't mean to do it." The bar on the door was swung clear, and the yachtsman pushed his way in.

Mikael was on his knees beside Marjatta, and the yachtsman gave a sigh of relief when he heard him say, "It isn't serious. It's only a scratch!"

"Only! ONLY!" Marjatta complained, angry at Mikael, but also ashamed at herself for screaming and almost fainting. But Mikael was right—the wound was little more than a scratch. A pellet from the shotgun had found a chink in the boards and, ricocheting through, had just cut the skin above Marjatta's right ankle. It was the roar of the gun and the sudden stinging pain which had shocked her into thinking she had really been shot. Angry at herself, she turned on her brother in a fury to demand, "You wouldn't have liked it, would you? It's all right for you to say it isn't serious. It hurts!" And her eyes filled with tears.

"I'm sorry," Mikael said soothingly. "I didn't mean that you were crying for nothing. I meant—"

"She's not dying, is she?" the old man said anxiously,

standing by the open door, looking past the yachtsman. His face was gray with worry.

The yachtsman turned on him in anger. "You were lucky you didn't kill her," he sputtered. "You . . . Oh! here, what have you got in that jug? If it's something to drink, bring it here. And you had better give me that gun before you do some more damage."

"I didn't mean to hurt anyone. . . . I wouldn't hurt a child for anything." The old man was shaken and frightened. He shuffled away to pick up the jug of coffee and the two mugs. "See," he said, as he picked the things up from the ground, "I was bringing them coffee when you came. If I didn't feel sorry for them I wouldn't have made coffee, would I? Is she badly hurt?"

"We'll have to get her home quickly," the yachtsman said, winking at Mikael and Marjatta. "Do you have a boat we could use?"

"Boat? No. My son-in-law, Timo, has the boat. He's gone for . . ." And there the old man stopped, and gulped.

"Gone for what?" the yachtsman insisted.

"I'll tell you where he's gone," Mikael said angrily. "He's gone to fetch the police. He was the one who stole our clothes during the night. He says that the *Red Dolphin* was stolen from Mariehamn harbor. They heard it on the radio, and there's a reward of five thousand Swedish crowns for whoever takes the yacht back to its owner."

The yachtsman's brows wrinkled in a deep frown. He took the jug of coffee from the old man, half filled one

of the mugs and handed it to Marjatta. He filled the
other mug and had almost put it to his lips when he
remembered Mikael.

"I'm sorry," he said, holding out the mug. "You drink.
There's plenty left."

"No sir, you drink. I'll wait. I can use Marjatta's cup."

"You say the *Red Dolphin* was stolen from Mariehamn
harbor," the yachtsman repeated after emptying the mug
to the last drop. "Who . . . who's supposed to have stolen
her?" He looked at Mikael, then at Marjatta, then at the
old man, who fidgeted and began to feel for his pipe.
After a moment's silence the yachtsman continued,
"Well, doesn't anyone know who stole the yacht? Am I
supposed to have stolen her?"

It was Mikael's turn to gulp and look down.

"I see," the yachtsman said, and shrugged. "I suppose
I can't blame you for thinking I stole her. Perhaps I did.
I don't know who I am or how I got the yacht. I don't
even know where I come from." He lifted a hand to his
swollen forehead and sighed. Then he turned to the old
man. "You say your son has gone for the police?"

"He's my son-in-law," the old man mumbled. "And he
hasn't gone for the police. He's gone to fetch some
friends to help him repair the yacht so he can take you
on it across to Mariehamn. Then the police can arrest
you, and he'll get the reward."

"Do you have a . . ." then the yachtsman stopped,
pushed past the old man, and picked up the fox terrier.
He had been crawling toward the shed and had managed
to get to his feet, only to wobble for a second, then fall

again. Scooped up by a strong hand, the dog soon lay with his head on the yachtsman's shoulder while a hand stroked him gently.

"Oh, we must do something for the dog!" Marjatta exclaimed. Forgetting her injury, she followed her brother into the open. "Please," she begged the old man, "we've got to help him." To the yachtsman she explained, "He saved me from an adder. I would have been bitten if not for him."

"An adder!" the yachtsman said. "They're poisonous, aren't they? Shouldn't he be dead by now?"

"Marjatta . . . my sister," Mikael nodded toward Marjatta, "cut the place and sucked at the wound, but she mustn't have got all the venom out."

"You can't do nothing about it here," the old man said, reaching out a hand to stroke the dog. "You must give him whisky, or some other spirit, and that's something we haven't got. You didn't suck all the poison out . . . so he'll just take longer to die, that's all."

"We can do something, surely," the yachtsman said briskly. "Isn't there a boat of any kind here? Surely you have a small boat—even a rowing boat."

"Nothing," the old man replied. "Timo just has his fishing boat. So the only other craft on the island is the yacht—the *Red Dolphin*. And it isn't any use hoping my son-in-law will help when he gets back. He won't have any time for the dog. He's got his eyes on that reward. Five thousand Swedish crowns is a lot of money. When he and his friends get here they'll probably lock you up while they repair the yacht. Then they'll sail the *Red Dolphin* across to Mariehamn, so he'll be sure to get the reward. He won't waste time on a sick dog."

"So the dog will die," the yachtsman said soberly, stroking the fox terrier gently down the back. "I don't like that. I just don't like it."

"You can't do anything to save him," the old man retorted. "What can you do? No boat; no whisky or brandy. You can't do anything."

Marjatta looked down at her bare feet. Her eyes swam with tears and she chewed on her lower lip. She blinked, and swallowed hard, trying to keep back the sob which was coming. After a moment of silence Mikael asked, "How long will it be before your son-in-law gets back, sir?"

"How many times will you call me *sir?*" the old man said irritably. "My name is Elias. I never was a sir, and at my age I'm never likely to be. I'm Elias. What do they call you?"

"I'm Mikael Ekman," Mikael said, "and my sister is Marjatta." Then he looked at the yachtsman, who smiled wryly and shrugged.

"I don't know what you'll call me," he admitted. Turning to the old man, he said, "Choose a name for me."

Elias scratched at his mop of gray hair for a moment. Suddenly his eyes gleamed. "How would Gustav do? I knew a Swedish fisherman once who was called Gustav, and I liked him."

"That'll suit me," the yachtsman agreed, smiling. "Call me Gustav. Now, Elias, Mikael was asking you how long it would be before your son-in-law got back here with his friends."

Elias combed his fingers through his beard thoughtfully. "Maybe another three hours. There isn't much wind, and he doesn't have an engine in his boat. Of course he might come back from the other island in a boat that has an engine. . . . then he would probably be here in two hours." Suddenly suspicious, he asked, "What do you want to know for?"

Race Against Time

6

MIKAEL DREW IN A DEEP BREATH, looked thoughtful for a moment, then said, "I was thinking we might be able to save the dog if we repaired the yacht. I looked at her this morning. Two of her starboard bow planks are smashed in, but if we had some sacking, tar, and planks, we might make her seaworthy."

"Oh, could we?" Marjatta looked up, her cheeks wet with tears. "Please, let's try. Anything is better than just doing nothing."

Gustav looked earnestly at Mikael. Then he turned to the old man. "Now, Elias, you are the one to help. What about it? Can you find tar and planks? If you could, we might do more than save the dog."

All eyes were on the old man whose brow was furrowed in a deep frown. Very slowly, he shook his head. Marjatta's eyes, which had brightened with hope, dulled again and the eager look in Mikael's eyes faded. If there was no tar and no planks, then there would be no hope of repairing the *Red Dolphin*.

It was the tall, fair-haired Gustav who raised their hopes after a moment or so by saying, "Elias, your son-in-law must repair his boat from time to time. Are you sure there is no tar, and equipment? Are you positively sure? Wait . . . don't answer yet, for I have something else to say."

He hitched up his blanket and retied the rope about his waist while Mikael, Marjatta, and Elias waited in silence. When the knot was tied to his satisfaction Gustav said, "Suppose we managed to mend the yacht and sailed her away. Suppose I took the dog ashore somewhere so that he could have medical care and you took the yacht on to Mariehamn. What would happen?"

He got no answer. Not only were the two youngsters puzzled, but Elias also, for he did not understand what Gustav was hinting at.

"Well, I'll tell you," Gustav said, as a little smile made the corners of his mouth twitch. "When you handed over the yacht at Mariehamn, whoever has offered five thousand Swedish crowns for her return would come aboard —and somebody would get that reward."

"Somebody?" And now there was a croak of excitement in the old man's voice. "You mean me?"

"You and these youngsters, if they stayed aboard with you," Gustav pointed out. "There would be sixteen hundred and some-odd Swedish crowns as your share, Elias. What could you do with so much money?"

The old man gulped, and his beard wagged up and down with excitement. "Sixteen hundred Swedish crowns! One thousand six hundred crowns! If I had that much money I could buy a steamer ticket and go to stay with my youngest daughter who lives in Denmark. Are you sure I would get so much?"

"What does three into five thousand come to, Mikael?"

Gustav asked, but it was Marjatta who answered. She had always been better at mental arithmetic than her brother.

Her voice was shrill with excitement as she shouted, "Three into five thousand is sixteen hundred and sixty-six and two thirds."

"Wait here," Elias said, and shuffled off. While he was gone Marjatta said, "Wouldn't it be better if you went to Mariehamn with the yacht, sir?"

"And give myself up to the police? I don't know." Gustav rubbed his chin thoughtfully. "I just can't imagine myself stealing a yacht, and yet how did I come to be on the *Red Dolphin?* Somebody stole it."

"But if you did go to Mariehamn, the police would know who you were, wouldn't they?" Mikael suggested. "I mean—perhaps they would be able to tell you who you are."

"I'll have to have time to think this out," Gustav said thoughtfully. "I agree, the quickest way of finding out who I am would be for me to go to Mariehamn. But suppose I am a thief. I'd be in prison before I knew what was happening."

Marjatta sighed. She was beginning to like Gustav, and the thought that he might be a thief worried her.

The tension was broken by the appearance of old Elias, carrying a saw and two short planks. Within five minutes they had almost everything they needed—a five-gallon drum of heavy tar, long nails, several pieces of stout sailcloth, and a brush with which to smear on the tar. Then Elias made a suggestion which his three new acquaintances welcomed:

"If you could spare five minutes, I could put some food out—and I'll warm a drop of condensed milk for the dog. It won't cure him, but it might keep his strength up a bit."

Together they went into the old house, and Elias went into the back room for bread and smoked herring. In an excited whisper Marjatta said, "Mikael, the wallet and notebook!" and pointed to a small shelf over the fireplace.

"My wallet!" Gustav's eyes gleamed, and a moment later he was opening the still wet notebook. At that moment the old man came back. He frowned, then shook his head, saying, " 'Taint no use trying to read what's in that. Timo tried; but the pages is that thin they're stuck together. You can't get 'em apart at all."

Gustav tried and tried to separate the ink-stained pages, but the paper was so thin that it was quite impossible; and on the front page the ink had run so badly that every word was blurred and unreadable.

"I'll say this of Timo, he isn't a thief," the old man said, putting a pan of water to boil for coffee. "Aint took nothin' out of the wallet. Just wanted to be sure he was right about you . . . but he might as well have saved his time. Nobody is ever going to read what was written in that little book . . . nobody."

Gustav shook his head and replaced wallet and notebook on the little shelf. Elias cut bread and laid out smoked herring. He made coffee, and though much more time than the five minutes they had planned passed before they were ready to leave, they all felt much better for the hurried meal. As they were about to leave, Mikael said, "I've thought of something else we'll need: a spade! The yacht ran her bow onto the beach, and we'll have to dig her clear or we'll never get her into deep water again."

"We have a spade," Elias assured them, and shuffled away again.

"You see what the prospect of money will do," Gustav said, smiling. "At first he told us there was no tar. Now he finds he has all manner of things."

"I don't think it's the money so much as the thought of getting away from his son-in-law," Marjatta said. "I feel sorry for him, don't you, Mikael?"

Mikael nodded. He was testing the weight of the tar drum, and pulling a face. It was heavy, and getting it across the half-mile-wide island to the beach where the *Red Dolphin* was stranded was not going to be easy.

Elias brought rope, and they knotted it into a sling so that two of them could carry the tar drum. Then, before they started for the western side of the island, Elias hurried into the house again and came back with an old-fashioned spyglass which he handed to Marjatta. He was bubbling over with excitement now and looking not at all like the tough old man he had seemed when the youngsters first met him.

"That spyglass belonged to a man who was captain of one of the old clipper ships. They were the ones that used to sail from Australia to Europe, loaded with grain," he informed them. "It's a good glass. While we men are working on the yacht, you've got to use the spyglass," he told Marjatta. "Know why?"

Marjatta shook her head. She could not think how

using a spyglass would help repair the *Red Dolphin*.

"Well, I'll tell you." Elias was chuckling now at his own cleverness. "When there is a chance of trouble coming, the wise ones always keep a good lookout. That's what I want you to do with the spyglass. If we have warning of when Timo is coming, we'll know what to do. You see, he'll have promised his friends a share of the reward and they'll be as eager as he is to lay their hands on you. I daresay he'll bring three or four with him. So we mustn't be caught napping, must we?"

Three heads nodded agreement. Now that there seemed a chance of repairing the *Red Dolphin* and getting away, the thought of being caught at the last moment sent little shivers through Marjatta and Mikael.

"There is one other thing," Gustav told Elias as he bent to pick up his share of the equipment to be carried over to the west beach. "What about our clothes? I'm not happy stalking about in a blanket. I feel as if I should be on a stage, acting in a play."

"Oh, the clothes. Hm!" The old man's face clouded for a moment. "It'll take a few minutes, and we don't know how long it will be before they come, do we?"

"I think we should have our clothes," Gustav insisted. "After all, if I decide to try to keep out of the way of the police, I'd look pretty silly running around dressed in a blanket."

"Come on, then." Elias led them back into the house and from a big chest brought out a great bundle of clothing. It was all knotted up with the rope on which the clothes had been hung to dry.

For the next few minutes the three sets of clothing

were untangled and sorted. Marjatta went into the back
room to dress, leaving her brother and Gustav to dress in
the front room. Although the clothes were badly creased
and still a little damp, Marjatta felt much better as she
smoothed out her dress. A blanket was not the sort of
garment she liked to wear.

"We'll leave the blankets here," Elias decided, and no
one argued. When they were outside again and looking
at the pile of equipment they had to carry over to the
west beach, he offered, "I'll carry the spade and the
planks if you can carry the rest."

Mikael and Gustav took the ropes on the drum of tar,
and each carried something under his other arm. Mikael
had the saw and a small bag of nails. Gustav had the
heavy hammer and a roll of tarpaulin. Marjatta was left
to bring along the spyglass and the little dog.

For some time the terrier had lain without movement,
though he did open his eyes and look up as Marjatta
lifted him gently into her arms. And his tail wagged
feebly as she stroked him and whispered encouragement.

Gustav and Mikael had the hardest task. When they
finally set down the tar drum on the beach a few yards
from the *Red Dolphin* their hands were red and the skin
on their fingers had been rubbed into painful ridges.

"You can't afford to rest," Elias warned. "Time to rub
your hands later. If Timo gets here before we get the
yacht into deep water, it's good-by to everything. The
dog won't get treatment, and you, Gustav, you'll end up
in prison."

"Slave driver, isn't he?" Gustav smiled ruefully.

"Trouble is, Elias, *you* didn't carry the tar drum. Anyway, I'm sure you're right." And he walked down to the water's edge to look at the yacht's damaged hull.

Marjatta laid the little dog down in the most comfortable place she could find. As she stroked him and spoke gently to him, his eyes opened, and he tried to lift his head to lick her hand.

"You poor, brave thing," Marjatta whispered. "Just lie and rest. We'll do everything we can to get help for you." She gave him a last, reassuring pat and went to ask Elias what she should do.

"We've got to have a fire to warm the tar so that it will brush on," he said. "You can fetch firewood while we cut the planks to fit the damaged hull."

Mikael shook his head in amazement. It was hard to imagine any man changing as much as Elias had changed in the past hour. He did not look to see if Marjatta started to carry out his orders but picked up one of the planks and carried it across to the *Red Dolphin*. There he began to measure where he would have to saw the wood to make a good patching job.

Marjatta climbed to the top of the cliff and gathered twigs and dead branches from beneath the pine and juniper trees. When she returned she saw that Mikael was busy with the saw. Gustav was hammering the top off the drum of tar and Elias was cutting the sheet of tarpaulin to the size required for the patch he planned to put on the damaged hull of the *Red Dolphin*.

Marjatta lighted the fire, then collected stones to build a little fireplace on which the tar drum could stand so

that it would heat and soften the tar. Then Elias ordered
her to go up to the nearest place from which she could
watch the sea to the northeast.

She had to walk halfway across the island before she
found a place high enough for her to see to the islands
lying to the northeast. She made sure there were no adders about. Then she removed the caps from the ends of
the spyglass and took her first look through it.

She was disappointed; the distant islands were a blur.
She tried lengthening the spyglass by pushing out the
outer barrel and found that things were very much

clearer. She could even see individual trees on the nearest island. The sea was a carpet of twinkling spots of color as tiny waves caught the sunlight. But she saw no signs of shipping on the sea—though she looked everywhere.

She adjusted the spyglass so that she could look at things closer to her. A hundred yards away a big herring gull was swooping down on something. She adjusted the spyglass so that she could watch him. "You horrid thing," she muttered as she saw the big gull swoop down on the nest of an eider duck.

She must have been hiding newly hatched ducklings under her downy plumage, for she raised herself up as the herring gull made his swoop, and jabbed upward at the thief. The gull flapped his wings and soared just out of reach, his slate-blue wings flashing in the sunlight.

Marjatta could see the gull's wicked-looking yellow beak as he swooped again. He meant to have one or two of the young goslings, but first he had to frighten the eider duck from her nest.

The herring gull attacked her five times and each time the mother eider met the attack with flapping wings and an upward thrust of her own black-topped head. The sixth time Marjatta bit her lip with anxiety as the mother eider remained crouched on the nest as if too tired or too frightened to meet the attack.

The screaming herring gull swept down once more in a relentless attack, but just when it seemed as if the duck would be killed, she moved. As if shot upward by a powerful spring, she rose off her nest.

Through the strong lens of the spyglass, Marjatta

watched the battle end. The herring gull tried to check his descent, but he was too late. The mother eider jabbed, and a moment later the gull fluttered away, trailing one wing. He did not return.

Suddenly remembering why she was there, Marjatta hurriedly adjusted her spyglass and looked across the sea to the distant islands. There was still nothing to see but bird life.

An hour later, made drowsy by the morning sun, Marjatta hurried back to the beach. First she went to the dog. When she stroked him he wagged his tail feebly and tried to lick her hand. She could see that he was still very sick. She sighed, and turned away to see what progress had been made on repairing the yacht.

She was disappointed. The tar had been softened over the fire. With the help of Mikael and Gustav, Elias was nailing a well-tarred piece of canvas over the damaged hull.

"How long will it take now?" Marjatta asked.

"Not long, not long," Elias assured her, wiping his face with the back of his right hand, leaving a smudge of tar across his cheek and the side of his beard. "Another hour will see a change."

Marjatta looked anxiously at her brother. He shrugged. Repairing the yacht was not as easy or as quick a job as he had thought it would be. It was clear, however, that Elias knew what he was doing and that when he had finished, the hull would be watertight. Whether they could get the *Red Dolphin* repaired and afloat before Elias's son-in-law returned was another matter.

"I wish they'd be quicker," Marjatta murmured. Then she rose and went back to her lookout point on the cliff. The sea was still empty, and remained so while another hour passed. Just as she was about to return to the beach, certain that the repair work must be finished, Marjatta saw the boat.

Adjusting the spyglass, she focused on it. There was one thing she could be sure of, it had a motor. She could see the little trail of white behind it as the froth, churned up by a propeller, showed against the shadow of the trees on the shore.

It was Timo and his friends! She was sure it must be. Elias had said that no ordinary fisherman would be out, for the herring would not come near the surface until sunset. Closing the spyglass, Marjatta ran back to the beach as quickly as she could. To her dismay the yacht looked as if no progress had been made on it. Mikael and Gustav were holding a piece of planking against the red hull while Elias was hammering at a long nail.

"They're coming!" Marjatta shrieked as she slithered down the last slope to the beach. "A boat just rounded one of the islands and it isn't sailing. It has a motor."

The three stopped work as Marjatta ran toward them panting for breath. Elias grunted with dismay.

"That's it," he said. He began to pull his fingers through his beard, forgetting he had been tarring. His tar-covered fingers stuck to the coarse gray hair. He tried to free them with his other hand, but that too was coated with tar. In seconds both hands were caught in his beard and refused to come free, and jerking them was painful.

He looked helplessly from Marjatta to Mikael to Gustav.

"Try pulling one finger at a time," Gustav suggested. "I'll help." But not only was the beard strong but the tar was sticking faster every second. Each time Gustav tried to free one of the old man's fingers, Elias gasped until his eyes brimmed with tears.

"I think a good jerk would do it," Mikael suggested. "You know: One-two-three, as if you were having a tooth out. Take a deep breath, close your eyes and then —*wuff*, and your hands will be free."

Elias took a deep breath, closed his eyes, and jerked. His mouth opened and he howled.

"We'll have to cut you free," Gustav said, holding out his hand for Mikael's knife. Elias groaned, insisting he would look funny without his beard.

"You'll look even funnier if you leave your hands stuck like that," Gustav pointed out. Taking Mikael's knife, he began to saw gently through the tarred beard. When he finished, the beard was a jagged, untidy mop. Groaning, Elias went over to the dying fire. Holding his hands over the flame to make the tar soften, he wiped the mass of gray hair from his fingers.

"It's taken me years to grow this beard," he groaned, "and I'll never live long enough to grow another as fine. A man without a beard—"

"Your son-in-law is coming," Marjatta reminded him. The grins quickly vanished from the faces of Mikael and Gustav. "Is there anything I can do?"

"Go up and watch," Gustav said. "If they steer as if they are coming around to this beach, come back right

away. Well, you had also better come immediately if
they put in at the other beach."

"Yes," Elias agreed. "Once Timo discovers I'm missing
and you're gone, too, he'll be here as fast as his legs will
carry him." As Elias spoke he gingerly stroked his ruined
beard. "We'll have to get the yacht into the water. If
she leaks, we'll just have to pump. Where's the spade?"

Marjatta hurried back to her lookout and was alarmed
to see how close the boat was. In a matter of minutes it
would be near enough for the men to wade ashore. They
would easily be at Timo's home within ten minutes after
landing. She began to run toward the beach, her heart
pounding with excitement and fear.

If Timo caught them, he certainly would not worry
about getting the dog to a doctor. His one thought would
be to make Gustav a prisoner, sail the yacht to Mariehamn and then collect the reward. Elias had told them
so.

When she got to the beach she closed her eyes in
despair. Mikael was shoveling pebbles from beneath the
bow of the *Red Dolphin*. Elias and Gustav were helping
by scraping them away with their hands.

"They're coming," she screamed. "The boat is putting
in at the beach near the house."

Elias looked up. He was panting, for he had been
scraping with all the strength he possessed. He was an
old man.

"Are you sure?" he wheezed.

"Of course I'm sure," Marjatta gasped. "Do you think
I would run here to tell you this if I weren't? They'll be
landing now."

"Is there time to get her off the beach?" Gustav asked. He sighed as the old man shook his head, sat down, and began to feel for his pipe.

"We'll need to move a lot more beach before she floats. It'll be half an hour before she'll budge," Elias lamented. "Ah, me," he groaned, "to be so near winning, and then to lose by a few minutes."

"Go and see if they've landed," Mikael urged Marjatta. "We can keep digging until they come."

"No!" Marjatta said. Then, turning to Elias, she scolded, "As my brother says, you can keep trying until they come. They're not actually here yet."

"She'll not move," Elias insisted. "I've worked fishing boats long enough to know when a boat is ready to slide off a beach. She's a dead weight, and she won't come off for . . ." He stopped speaking as Marjatta pushed past him and began to scramble onto the yacht. "What do you think you are going to do?" he asked in sudden anger. "Lift the yacht into the sea barehanded?"

There was so much scorn in his voice that Marjatta was about to snap back at him. But he was an old man and probably thought that girls were quite useless when it came to dealing with boats. So, quietly she said, "No, I'm not going to try to push the yacht into the sea, but it might help if we could start the motor. With the propeller trying to pull her astern something might happen. What do you think?"

Desperate Encounter

7

IF MARJATTA HAD SAID THE YACHT was already afloat her words could not have had a more startling effect. Gustav closed his eyes and an expression of disgust at his own stupidity in not thinking of the motor crept over his face. Mikael's mouth opened in astonishment. He had often been proud of his sister, but never more than now.

Old Elias, who had been about to start scraping in his pipe bowl with his knife blade, looked as if he had been stung. His head jerked up; the knife was shut with a resounding *click.* "*Aough!* Doesn't that just show how you should never be too sure. What an old fool I am! I should have thought of that earlier. The stern is in deep water. The propeller can turn, and if the engine was run at full speed maybe we *could* get her off the beach. Here, help me up."

Marjatta was already climbing onto the deck. Mikael helped Elias up, while Gustav splashed into the water amidships and climbed aboard there.

"I'll scrape more pebbles from under her while you start the engine," Mikael shouted. Grabbing the spade without waiting for anyone to agree with his suggestion,

he began digging. Spadeful after spadeful of pebbles
flew from under the *Red Dolphin's* keel.

Marjatta's idea had given them all new hope. Yet
when they stood looking at the green-painted diesel
engine some of the excitement faded. No one knew
how to start the engine. Marjatta had thought Gustav
would know, for he had been on the *Red Dolphin* when
it chugged along under engine power. But he shook his
head.

"I suppose I ought to know," he admitted sadly. "After
all, if I stole the boat, and was bringing her out here
under engine power, I must have started the dratted
engine, but—I've forgotten who I am. So I suppose I can
be forgiven for having forgotten how to start the engine."

"You've been a fisherman," Marjatta said, turning to
Elias. "You must know, surely."

"When I was a sailor, nobody could afford things like
engines. We used sails," the old man said soberly. "Pull
one of them levers and see what happens."

"That makes the engine go faster or slower," Marjatta
said, laying a hand on the throttle lever. She pushed it
forward, then pulled it back. But the engine remained
dead.

Gustav reached out to a small wheel and turned it.
All three jumped nervously. There was a sudden *thump-
thump-thump* from the engine. Gustav had turned on
the compressed air which worked the starter motor.
For perhaps half a minute the engine turned over, labor-
ing heavily. Then, with a sudden terrific *bang*, the engine
started.

For a full minute it ran unevenly, threatening to stop. Cautiously Gustav pushed the throttle lever forward a little, and at once the engine speed increased.

"Something should happen now," Elias said excitedly.

"I think you have to do something with that," Marjatta suggested, pointing to the gear lever. "You do it. I'm frightened." She appealed to Gustav.

He was about to move it when he noticed some lettering where the lever went down through a slot. There were two words, each next to a small arrow: *Forward* and *Reverse*. He pushed it gently in the direction of the *Reverse* arrow. After a crunch of gears, there was a sudden slowing down of the engine speed. It was now turning the propeller.

Marjatta pushed the throttle lever forward a little more, and the engine speed picked up. All three climbed onto the stern and looked down. Foam was churning up from the unseen propeller.

As they watched it, Mikael shouted: "Come here and lend a hand. I think she'll move with a bit of help."

"You stay on board," Gustav told Elias. "If she gets into the water you might not be able to get back on her."

Marjatta jumped down to the beach with Gustav at her heels. At a yell from Mikael they all heaved. They could feel the thrumming of the engine as they leaned their weight against the red planking. *Thrum-thrum-thrum-thrum;* but there was no seaward movement of the *Red Dolphin*. To Marjatta it seemed as if it were locked onto the pebbled beach.

She heard her brother scream to Elias, "Open the throttle more. Give her more power."

They pushed and waited, and to their horror, instead of the engine roaring more loudly, it suddenly began to splutter unevenly, and then died away. It left a stillness in which each of them could hear the beating of his racing heart.

"Start it up again," Gustav bellowed.

A moment later Mikael was yelling, "Push, push . . . I think she's moving. Push! Push! PUSH!"

Even Marjatta got the feel of it—a faint quivering ran through the *Red Dolphin* as its keel grated over the pebbles. The yacht must have been quite finely balanced on the slanting beach, and the throbbing as the engine roared in reverse had finally broken the beach's grip. Now, as Mikael, Marjatta, and Gustav continued to push, the red yacht began to slide slowly down the beach and into the deep water.

The last few feet were terrible for them all. As the stern lifted with the water under it, the yacht's bow tried to dig into the pebbles. The movement grew slower, and threatened to cease altogether.

Then came a yell from Elias. "They're here!" he roared. "They're coming down to the beach. Come on —PUSH!"

"PUSH!" It sounded like one voice as Marjatta, Mikael, and Gustav shouted the command together. Somehow they found more strength. Pebbles slipped from beneath their straining feet. They bruised their shoulders against the woodwork of the *Red Dolphin;* yet the yacht would not budge.

Then, unexpectedly, there was a renewal of the *crunch-crunch-crunch* of pebbles under the keel, and the *Red Dolphin* now seemed to be in a hurry, sliding the last few feet. The bow dipped in a wild curtsy— and the *Red Dolphin* was afloat. Afloat and beginning to move into deeper water.

There was no chance for Mikael, Marjatta, and Gustav to wade out to the boat. They would have to swim. Boldly they plunged in after the *Red Dolphin* as it moved gently farther and farther from the beach.

They were just in time. Timo and his four friends had just reached the churned-up gravel where the yacht had been only a minute or so earlier. There they stood, yelling angrily as Timo roared threats at Elias, ordering him to return.

The old man was too busy helping Marjatta aboard to pay attention to his son-in-law. Mikael managed to climb onto the *Red Dolphin* unaided. Then he flopped face down on deck, breathless and exhausted. Gustav, once aboard, was also too worn out to do more than remain on his knees, gasping. But Elias, an impish grin on his face, danced excitedly in the *Red Dolphin's* bow. "I've finished with you, my lad, finished," he roared at Timo. "When I get my share of the five thousand Swedish crowns I'll be off to Denmark as fast as a ship can take me. My daughter will look after me."

"Traitor," Timo cried, shaking his fist angrily. "After all I've done for you. But you'll not get away with it. Come on, lads. We'll soon catch them in our boat." They turned and ran back up the bank.

"They'll never catch us," Elias chuckled. He patted

Marjatta on the shoulder. His smile faded as he realized that the girl's clothing was soaking wet. "You'd better get down into the cabin and wring the water out of your clothes," he told her. "The others can do the same later."

Marjatta nodded, then turned to see how her brother was, knowing how difficult an unaided climb from the sea onto a moving yacht could be. Mikael was still gasping.

"Are you all right?" Marjatta asked anxiously.

Mikael wiped a wet hand over his face, then pushed hair from his forehead. He grinned as he got to his feet. But suddenly the grin vanished. "Marjatta," he asked, "where is the dog?"

The dog! In the excitement all thought of the dog had been driven from her mind. She frowned, trying to think where she had last seen him. Then she gave a sudden wail of despair. "We've left him. I can see him, there, on the beach." She pointed. "We'll have to go back." The *Red Dolphin* was now twenty yards from the shore, and a gentle wind was beginning to turn it around, urging it to head for the open sea.

"Don't worry," Mikael soothed. He yelled to Elias to start the engine so that they could go inshore to pick up the dog. Only then did Elias tell them that he had not stopped the engine. It had begun to splutter and had stopped of its own accord.

"I wasn't even looking at it when it stopped," the old man protested. "Gustav started the engine. He knows how."

Gustav, looking very tired, did what he had done earlier. He turned the little valve wheel which allowed compressed air to rush to the starter motor. Again the engine turned over with a sullen *clump-bumpity-thump*, but there was no heartening thunder to show that the engine had started. And the *Red Dolphin* continued to drift farther and farther from the beach.

"Look, we should be getting the sails up," Elias reminded them anxiously. "If we don't get away quickly that son-in-law of mine will be here with his friends and then we'll be in real trouble. It'll be worse for me than for anybody."

"I'll swim ashore," Marjatta offered desperately. "We can't leave the dog behind, and I—"

"*You* aren't swimming anywhere," Mikael said firmly as he tore off his sodden jacket. "Find a rope in case I have any trouble getting back." Before Marjatta could protest he dived over the side. Quickly she found a long length of rope, and made a loop in one end.

Exhausted, Mikael yelled to Marjatta to throw him the rope. It splashed into the sea only a yard or so from him. When he reached the dog he looked very tired. He slipped the loop around his waist. Then, with the dog sitting on his chest, he began to swim on his back toward the *Red Dolphin*.

Meanwhile old Elias had been loosening the big sail. There was a light breeze, and a yacht like the *Red Dolphin* needed only a capful of wind to send it skimming along.

The moment boy and dog were safely aboard, Elias

and Gustav hoisted the mainsail. That done, the old man
went to the tiller. For a moment or so the *Red Dolphin's*
sail flapped noisily, then as the boat turned under the
effect of the rudder, the sail gently filled.

Old man though he was, and retired from the sea for
a number of years, Elias had not forgotten how to handle
a sailing boat. He sat in the stern, nursing the tiller, and
steering the *Red Dolphin* so cleverly that it caught every
little puff of wind.

Marjatta rubbed down the fox terrier with part of a
sheet she had found in one of the lockers in the cabin.
Meanwhile Mikael went into the far cabin and, stripping
off his clothes, wrung as much water from them as he
could. Gustav did the same. Marjatta was the last to
go in the forward cabin. She put even more wrinkles
in her clothes as she wrung every possible drop of water
from them.

She came on deck feeling better and was about to
ask if she should try to make something hot for them all
to drink. But Elias, Mikael, and Gustav were staring
anxiously astern. There was no need to ask why they
were frowning. About a mile away was a fishing boat.
Its mast carried no sail, but there was a splash of white
water at its bow, showing that, driven by a motor, it
was coming along at a good speed.

"Is that the one?" Mikael asked Marjatta, knowing
that she had seen the boat which had brought Timo
and his friends from the other island. Marjatta needed
no powerful spyglass this time. Even at this distance
she recognized the pursuing craft. It was Timo's boat.

"They're overtaking us," Gustav said soberly. "How many are there? I'm afraid I was too exhausted to notice. I heard the shouting, and guessed it must be your son-in-law from the things you yelled at him."

"Yes, it was Timo," Elias said angrily. "And he brought enough of his friends to make sure you'd be captured and the yacht repaired. Hasn't got the heart of a chicken. If there had been a fight he would have been at the back."

"How many are there with him?" Gustav repeated his question.

"Five, counting Timo." Elias did not hide his disgust. "Five grown men to capture one man. Humph!"

"Five!" Gustav repeated the word and shrugged. "We can't beat five. If they catch up with us, well . . ." and he shrugged again.

For a quarter of an hour nothing more was said. Marjatta had forgotten her idea of trying to make a hot drink. The yacht was sailing beautifully, but it was being overtaken. The powerful engine in the fishing boat was bringing Timo and his friends nearer and nearer.

Elias had turned the tiller over to Gustav and then hoisted the small bowsprit. But even that triangular sail could not give them the speed they needed. When the pursuing boat was about three hundred yards away Mikael suddenly grabbed Gustav by the arm. "If you swing to the left, between those rocks," he said excitedly, "we'll be able to head straight for our island. If we can get there, my mother will help us deal with this gang."

"Deal with five men!" Gustav raised his eyebrows to show he found this hard to believe. However, he put the tiller over, and the *Red Dolphin* heeled gracefully as it turned.

"It will take more than a woman to put my son-in-law off," Elias said crossly. "He thinks he's helping the law—and he wants the reward."

"You don't know our mother," Marjatta said firmly.

"You should hear some of the stories she tells about when she was a nurse at the time of the war between Finland and Russia," Mikael said warmly. "She can fight, I tell you. And she isn't afraid of anyone."

"Can we get between those rocks?" Gustav asked. The space between the two wicked-looking black rocks seemed very small.

"Let me have the tiller," Mikael pleaded. "I've sailed between them many times. And I think I know how to finish Timo and his friends."

"Finish them?" Gustav sounded doubtful. "What do you mean?"

"Well, you can see they've hoisted their big sail, and they're coming up much quicker now," Mikael said. "Once we're through the gap between the rocks, I'm going to put my tiller over and swing to the right. They'll have to do the same . . . and there's a hidden reef just beyond. They'll go on the rocks and—"

"No, no, no," Gustav said hurriedly. "You wouldn't want anyone to be drowned, would you?"

"They can swim! Everybody can," Mikael protested.

Gustav shook his head. "I can swim," he said. "But I don't think I could swim ashore from here. Don't try to force them onto the rocks."

"We'll be caught," Mikael protested. But secretly he

was glad Gustav had refused to let him wreck the fishing boat.

Mikael steered with the skill of a real islander, and they skimmed without trouble between the two black rocks. Then the pursuing fishing boat drew near. Standing in its bow, Timo yelled at the old man, "You ungrateful rogue, if you think you are going to get the reward you're wrong. We're coming alongside, and if you resist you'll get your head cracked." Then he waved a boat hook.

There was no reply from the *Red Dolphin*. Marjatta sat in the stern with Mikael. Elias was chewing on his old pipe, his eyes puckered, a worried look on his face. He wondered what life would be like for him if Timo were to catch them.

The fishing boat, a curl of white foam at its blunt bow, came swinging nearer and Timo stood with his boat hook ready. Once within range he would reach out, hook onto the *Red Dolphin*—and the two vessels would be locked. Like Timo, the others were fishermen, and it would not be difficult for them to board the yacht.

Elias looked at Gustav, but he seemed to be staring into space. Soon the fishing boat was near enough for Timo to push out the boat hook and hook onto the yacht's low rail. The two vessels drew closer. One of Timo's companions took the boat hook, and Timo reached out toward the yacht's rail. He was poised for a leap which would take him onto the *Red Dolphin*.

Then Gustav moved. As Timo's hands closed over the

yacht's rail, Gustav lifted a foot. With a yell Timo with-
drew his hands, mumbling abuse as he sucked at his
bruised knuckles.

"Try it again, and you'll get the same treatment,"
Gustav shouted angrily. "You should know that you
cannot board another vessel without permission, unless
you are a police officer."

Yacht and fishing boat were now within the last hundred yards of the island beach. Timo and his friends
knew it must be now or never. If the *Red Dolphin* got
to the island, their chance of claiming the reward was
gone. The tiller was put over; the fishing boat drew
away, then surged on again, its powerful engine forcing
it past the yacht.

"They're going to try and stop us," Marjatta screamed.
Hurrying to the bow, she cupped her hands about her
mouth and shouted at the top of her lungs: "Mother
. . . Mother . . . MOTHER!"

She could see their house, set against the pine trees,
but there was no sign of life. Her mother, she knew,
might be working in the garden at the back of the house,
or milking the goats. If she was, and if the wind was
rustling the pines, she would not hear a scream from a
hundred yards out at sea.

After one last frantic scream Marjatta dropped to her
knees. The fishing boat, handled with skill, had come at
an angle across the bow of the *Red Dolphin*. Mikael had
put his tiller over, and the yacht had started to swing
away to the left. But the motor-driven fishing boat was
too quick.

Yells of anger came from the *Red Dolphin's* stern as Mikael, Elias, and Gustav saw what was bound to happen. Then came a report like a gunshot as the yacht's slender bowsprit snapped after striking the bow of the fishing boat. A few seconds later the two boats collided.

The fishing boat was heavier than the *Red Dolphin,* and sturdier. The yacht shivered under the impact, then heeled over until it seemed as if it would capsize. Had Marjatta not been on her knees and hanging on like a limpet, she would have been thrown into the sea.

Seconds after the collision, there was an even louder *bang* as the *Red Dolphin's* tall mast broke off. It fell to the left, the sail coming down with it like a flapping blanket which settled over the stern and covered Gustav, Elias, and Mikael.

Swinging gracefully back on an even keel, the *Red Dolphin* wallowed from side to side for a few moments, then settled down. Then three men, with Timo in the lead, scrambled onto its bow.

The shore was still sixty yards away. Timo had won!

Surprise Outcome

8

THE HEAVY MAINSAIL flapped and heaved as Mikael, Gustav, and old Elias tried to find their way out of its imprisoning folds. Marjatta grabbed a loop on the canvas and tried to lift the sail. Almost at once the little dog came out, his tail down and his legs trembling.

"Oh, you poor thing!" Marjatta was stooping to pick him up when two strong hands grabbed her from behind.

"You leave this to us," one of Timo's friends urged. When Marjatta struggled frantically to free herself, he warned her, "You'll only tire yourself, and we're not going to hurt you. We know you're not the thief. Come on . . . come on, now." The powerful man handled Marjatta with great gentleness as he guided her toward the bow. There she was handed over to two of the crew who had been left in the fishing boat. Marjatta was forced to sit on a locker, the little dog on her knees. She watched the two men fasten a stout rope to the *Red Dolphin*, and realized that they planned to tow the yacht away.

Stroking the dog, Marjatta saw Timo and a helper

heave at the heavy canvas sail and drag Mikael out. He was hustled onto the fishing boat where he was told to sit beside his sister.

"To be so near," Mikael groaned. "If we—"

"They've gotten Elias out," Marjatta interrupted.

A minute later the old man was taken off the *Red Dolphin* and put onto the fishing boat. He looked so unhappy that Marjatta laid a comforting arm across his shoulders. "It may not be as bad as you think, Mr. Elias," she told him.

The old man shook his head dolefully and was about to say something in reply, when from the shore came the sudden roar of a motorboat engine. In the confusion and excitement following the collision no one had even looked shoreward. Now all eyes turned to see a launch with several people aboard heading out toward them.

Timo and a friend were making frantic efforts to raise the last heavy heap of canvas under which Gustav was held prisoner when Marjatta gave a scream of delight. She had been staring hard at the approaching launch. Now she stood up shouting, "Mother . . . Mother!" Turning to Mikael, she said, "Mother is in the boat. Can you see her?"

Mikael, too, had been staring, and frowning. "Of course I can see her," he agreed. But he wondered why the others in the boat were from the Finnish police. Had something terrible happened at home?

A few moments later the beautifully varnished launch came alongside. Ana Ekman gave a scream of delight as she scrambled aboard the fishing boat and embraced her son and daughter in a hug which almost took their breath away.

"Where have you been?" Tears were streaming down their mother's face. Sitting down, she lifted the hem of her apron to dry her eyes. "I've been going mad, wondering what had happened to you. We all thought you were dead."

"Dead!" Mikael and Marjatta echoed the word, and exchanged startled glances.

"Look, ma'am, they're not dead." It was the sergeant of police, who had now climbed aboard the fishing boat. "We can hear their story later. For the moment I'm

concerned about this red yacht. Who is in charge here?
Who was on the yacht?"

From the deck of the *Red Dolphin* Timo called loudly,
"I'm in charge, sergeant. I don't know whether you saw
the little accident we had . . . but we have been chasing
the yacht. You've seen her name, I suppose. She's the
Red Dolphin—the yacht that was stolen from Mariehamn.
I heard the radio appeal. We were trying to catch her
and capture the thief when we collided. Anyway, I got
the yacht, and there's the thief." He pointed to Gustav,
who was now sitting on the folds of sail canvas, trying
to regain his breath.

"You had better come aboard the launch," the sergeant said sternly. "And I don't want to hear anything
more from anybody until we get ashore."

The motorboat towed the fishing boat and the *Red
Dolphin* into the shallows. Neither boat had suffered
serious damage from the collision, so neither was in
danger of sinking.

When the three vessels lay in the shallows, held se-
curely with anchors taken up beach and dug into the
sand, the police sergeant directed everyone ashore and
into the Ekman house.

"We'll hear your story first," the sergeant said, nodding at Mikael and Marjatta. "Were you kidnapped?"

"They couldn't have been kidnapped," Timo said
angrily. "They were working hand in glove with him,"
and he pointed to Gustav.

"I don't believe that," Ana Ekman said angrily. "The
wreckage of their boat was picked up, and it had ob-

viously been run down by a larger vessel. We were sure they had been drowned. How you can say they would work hand-in-glove with a thief, I just don't know."

"We picked up the boat," the police sergeant said, looking around at the roomful of people. "A big search has been going on for the missing yacht *Red Dolphin*. The wrecked dinghy carried the owner's name and island, so we brought it here. Mrs. Ekman hoped that her children had stayed the night with their father. Now we know they did not. So, what have you got to say about it?" He turned to Gustav.

"But you haven't heard our story," Mikael said, while Marjatta sat with head bowed, cuddling the little dog and gently stroking its back.

"All right, go on. And I want nothing but the truth," the sergeant said.

So, while the others remained silent, Mikael told their story. But when he got to the part where their attention had been attracted to the red yacht by the frantic barking of the dog, the police sergeant stopped him.

"Before we go any further," he said, taking his notebook from his pocket and studying some writing there, "let me find out one thing. Whom does this dog belong to?" He looked around at the people assembled in the Ekman dining room. One after the other they all denied owning the dog.

The sergeant rubbed his chin thoughtfully. "According to the statement issued by the Swedish police," he said, "there was a dog aboard the yacht. It was a pedigreed fox terrier valued at four thousand Swedish crowns. It was owned by a Mr. Per Magnussen, a Swedish millionaire, who was also the owner of the yacht. Now . . . Yes, sir, you were about to say something?" He looked across at Gustav, who had seemed startled by the name Per Magnussen.

Eyes closed, and with one hand on his forehead, Gustav whispered the name Per Magnussen several times. Finally he opened his eyes, looked across at the dog in Marjatta's arms and whispered hesitantly, "Bodo . . . Bodo . . . Come here, Bodo."

The effect was electrical. The dog, who had been lying quietly, gave a shrill yap of joy, struggled from Marjatta's grasp, and flopped weakly to the floor.

Marjatta bent to pick him up, but he staggered to his feet and with his tail wagging feebly, somehow got across the floor to Gustav. There he stood whimpering with excitement as he stared up at Gustav.

"It almost looks as if he's your dog," the police sergeant said gravely. "Is he?"

Again Gustav lifted a hand to his head. The dog was licking the fingers of his other hand with joy.

"I don't know. I just don't know what's been happening," Gustav whispered. "My head seems all wooly. I'm trying to remember something, but I don't know what."

Everyone waited, but Gustav finally shook his head wearily. For some reason the name Bodo had come into his mind when the dog was mentioned, but he could not think why, nor could he remember who he was, or where he came from.

"Maybe you'll remember later. In the meantime I

want a written statement from everyone," the sergeant said. "You will all tell your story individually to my constables. And while you are waiting to give your stories I don't want you talking to one another about what has happened."

"Would you like me to make some coffee, sergeant?" Ana Ekman asked. When her offer was accepted, the sergeant followed her into the kitchen.

Closing the door he said, "Mrs. Ekman, since you don't have a radio set you can't know what has been going on. I'll tell you, because you may be able to convince your children to tell you something they might not want to reveal to the police. This Mr. Per Magnussen I mentioned is a Swedish shipping magnate. He sent his yacht—the one we have on the beach here, the *Red Dolphin*—around to Mariehamn so that he could have a few days sailing between Aland and the coast of Finland."

He paused while Ana Ekman pumped water for her kettle. When the kettle was safely on the stove the sergeant went on, "Mr. Magnussen flew to Mariehamn in his own private plane. From that moment he vanished. When his yacht disappeared it was thought that he had been kidnapped. There was a radio set on board and it was Mr. Magnussen's practice when on holiday to contact his office with it every morning. This man who calls himself Gustav *could* be the missing Mr. Magnussen. The dog obviously knows him and yet . . ." The sergeant shook his head and shrugged.

"My children don't tell lies, sergeant," Ana Ekman

said quietly. "Let me see what I can get out of them. Perhaps you would let me have Marjatta in here to help . . . and I'll talk to her."

"Yes, do that. In the meantime I'm going to radio our headquarters at Turku and get them to contact Stockholm police headquarters."

After Ana had spoken to Marjatta she told the police sergeant that her daughter's story was straightforward and that she could offer no explanation.

Getting a statement from everyone was a long business. As the last statement was being taken, a Swedish helicopter arrived. It hovered like a huge dragonfly over the beach, then came down to make a perfect landing. The police sergeant went to meet the men from the helicopter, and brought one of them back to the house.

Gustav was sitting quietly at the table. Bodo was lying across his knees, dozing. Mrs. Ekman had given the little dog a mixture of milk and whisky to strengthen him. The man with the police sergeant gave Gustav a little bow, saying, "Good day, sir. How are you?"

For a moment Gustav looked at him, his eyes slowly widening with astonishment. Then, to the amazement of the others, he asked, "What are you doing here, Wulfson? I thought I left word . . ." and there his voice faltered. He looked around the room, lifted a hand to his forehead, and muttered, "Where am I? Wulfson, what's been happening? I'm all confused. What am I doing here?"

"That's what we want to know, sir. Everybody has been looking for you," Wulfson said quietly. "Did you take your yacht out from Mariehamn, as planned?"

Again Gustav's hand went to his forehead, and again there was a long pause before he said, "Yes, of course I did. Yes, I remember now, I was most annoyed to discover there was not even a watchman aboard the *Red Dolphin*. Since they were apparently not expecting me until the next morning I decided the crew was probably spending the evening ashore. I gave my dog Bodo some food, then took the yacht out to sea to get in an hour's sailing before sunset."

"And why didn't you come back, sir?" Wulfson asked.

"Come back? Didn't I return? I . . ." For a minute or more there was silence. Then, as if his memory were returning, Gustav looked up again and nodded. "Yes, I remember now," he said. "I set the automatic steering, and with the engine at half throttle went below to make a cup of coffee."

"And then?" Wulfson prompted as Gustav stopped once more, his brow crinkled in a deep frown.

"I don't know," was the puzzled reply. "I remember turning on the calor gas. I remember striking a match. Yes, I remember doing that, for I had to get a box from the locker, since I don't smoke and never carry matches. I remember striking the match—but I don't seem to recollect what happened afterward." He stared into space, frowning deeply. Finally he looked up and said, "No, I just can't remember anything after that."

"Don't you remember these people, sir?" Wulfson asked, indicating Marjatta, Mikael, and old Elias. Marjatta smiled, certain that Gustav's eyes would light up at once; but she gaped in amazement as the seconds ticked by and he said nothing. He stared at her, then at

Mikael, then at the old man. The fair-haired man whom
they had all known as Gustav, but who now seemed to
be a very important man named Per Magnussen, stared
and stared, then finally shook his head.

"I'm sorry, Wulfson. Should I know them? So far as
I can recollect I have never seen them in my life before.
Who are they?"

"Well, I—" Mikael began indignantly, but held back
the rest of what he was going to say when Marjatta gave
his hand a quick squeeze.

"We'll take you back to Mariehamn, sir," Wulfson
said quietly. "Doctor Leiktiff will be there now, and I
know he would like to give you a check-up. I'll arrange
for a Mariehamn boat to come over and tow the *Red
Dolphin* back for repairs."

As he was leading Mr. Per Magnussen to the door
Wulfson looked back for a moment and said, "I'm sorry
to leave you like this—without more than a word of
thanks, but you will be hearing from us very soon."

The police sergeant went down the beach to the helicopter and saw Wulfson and Mr. Magnussen aboard.
Five minutes later the machine was winging its way
across the sea, its rotor blades sending a loud *chack-
chack-ack-ack* across the quiet air.

When he returned to the house the sergeant said,
"Mr. Wulfson has asked me to say again how sorry he
is not to be able to stay longer, but it is very important
for Mr. Magnussen to be seen by a doctor as quickly
as possible. And don't worry about his not knowing you.
It seems obvious to me that the calor gas stove must

have exploded. I suppose he could have been struck by a fragment of metal. Whatever happened, it evidently caused loss of memory."

"His head was badly bruised when we first saw him," Mikael volunteered. "He looked terrible."

"I noticed the bruise," the sergeant said. "The queer thing about loss of memory is that often when memory comes back the affected person doesn't know what happened in between. When he saw Mr. Wulfson, who is one of his executives in Stockholm, he suddenly remembered him and then didn't know you. Anyway, I'm sure you won't be sorry you helped him. Mr. Wulfson assured me of that. And, of course, there is the reward for the yacht *Red Dolphin*."

"And what about us?" Timo asked sulkily. "Where do we come in? We helped."

The police sergeant shrugged. "I don't know that you can expect anything," he said. "After all, Mikael and Marjatta Ekman did the work. You may have thought you were helping, but did you really help? I don't think so."

Dejectedly Timo and his four friends went back to their boat. Old Elias watched them sail away, then turned sadly to Mikael and Marjatta. "And where do I go now?" he asked. "Timo won't take me back."

"Well, if there is a reward, you should share it," Marjatta assured him. "He did help us all he could," she said to her mother.

"You had better stay with us for a few days," Mrs. Ekman said, smiling warmly at Elias. "We have a spare

bed, and I don't think we shall miss the food you will
eat. Sit down, and I'll see if there is any of my husband's
tobacco about."

Elias was so overcome at this kindness that he could
not even stammer his thanks; he was blinking hard to
keep back the tears.

Mikael laid a hand on the old man's shoulder. "Don't
worry, Elias," he said. "I am sure everything will come
out all right. It usually does, doesn't it, Marj?"

"It will this time, I'm sure," Marjatta agreed. "And
I'm certain that Gustav won't forget you."

She was right. A week later an invitation came from
Mr. Per Magnussen for the Ekmans and Elias to spend
a few days with him in Stockholm. There was tremendous excitement in the time which followed as they prepared for the trip. Clothes were washed and pressed,
and a new pair of shoes bought for Elias.

The helicopter arrived on the day Mr. Magnussen had
set, and carried five passengers out across the sunlit
Baltic, over the Aland Islands' port of Mariehamn, and
on to the coast of Sweden and the beautiful city of
Stockholm. Mr. Magnussen was waiting for them in a
huge American car, driven by a chauffeur in a smart
uniform.

Any worries they had that Mr. Magnussen might not
recognize them vanished immediately, for he raised his
hat to Mr. and Mrs. Ekman, nodded and smiled at old
Elias, then held out his arms to Mikael and Marjatta.
In a warm, welcoming voice he said, "It was a day or

so before my head cleared properly, but I have remembered everything. You were very wonderful. Mr. and Mrs. Ekman, you have two very amazing children, and I shall never forget what they did for me, never." Then he stood aside and motioned them into the car.

After a meal at Mr. Magnussen's beautiful villa they were taken for a ride around the city, and then for a trip in one of Stockholm's many water taxis.

To round off the day, their host took them to one of the city's twin skyscrapers. By express lift, which made Marjatta grab at Mikael's arm, and brought a gasp from old Elias and a squeak from Ana Ekman, they sped skyward to a restaurant on the top floor, which seemed to the islanders to be halfway to heaven.

There, as dusk fell, they could look over the great city, built on a number of islands. Stockholm seemed then to be a carpet of millions of twinkling lights—motorcars carrying people home; traffic lights; neon advertising lights; residence, shop, and hotel lights.

As they sat down for the evening meal a man arrived carrying Bodo. They had not seen the dog earlier, Mr. Magnussen told them, because he had been in the care of a veterinarian. Yelping with excitement, Bodo flung himself into Marjatta's arms. For a few minutes the meal was delayed while Mikael and even Elias fondled the dog. That evening was an occasion none of them would ever forget.

For two more days they were shown around Stockholm by Mr. Magnussen or one of his staff. For the first time they went to the cinema and had the strange experience of sitting in the gloom and seeing things happen on the huge screen—and all in natural color.

On the evening before the day they were to leave Stockholm, Mr. Magnussen told Mikael and Marjatta that when they got back to their island they would find on the beach a boat similar to the one which the *Red Dolphin* had smashed. It was a present from him to them.

He gave Elias an envelope containing money, a boat ticket from Stockholm to Copenhagen and a railway ticket from Copenhagen to the little town where the old man's daughter lived.

"And don't worry about anything," Mr. Magnussen said, clapping a reassuring hand on Elias's shoulders. "When you reach Copenhagen there will be someone to meet you and take you to the train. At the other end your daughter will be waiting for you."

For a few moments the old man could only gape. Finally he stammered, "But how did you know where my daughter lives?"

Chuckling, Mr. Magnussen said, "One of the advantages of being a rich man is that you can get people to find out things for you. I've even been in touch with your daughter, and she's not only expecting you, but is looking forward to having you live with her and her husband."

It seemed as if Mr. Magnussen had thought of everything. He told Mr. and Mrs. Ekman that if their son Mikael ever wanted to become a ship's officer there would be a place for him in the Training School for

Officers for the Magnussen Line merchant ships. As for Marjatta, if she wanted to train to become a teacher, typist, secretary, hair stylist, or any of the things young women did, a word to Mr. Magnussen would make it possible.

Finally, an envelope was pressed into Mr. Ekman's hand. Quietly Mr. Magnussen said, "I value my life very highly, Mr. Ekman. Your son and daughter saved me. What I have put in this envelope will, I hope, help to make life more comfortable for you and Mrs. Ekman and your children."

The next morning they were driven to the docks, for old Elias was to sail on the morning tide. At the ship, when all who were not sailing were going ashore, Elias pulled an envelope from his pocket and gave it to Mikael. "I'd be glad if you would find a way of getting this to my son-in-law Timo," he said. "It's part of the money Mr. Magnussen gave me. I have all I'll ever need, and though I said some hard things about Timo, he did give me a home. And my address is in the envelope, too. Maybe Timo will invite me back to the island for a holiday sometime. I'm going to find it hard not to live by the sea."

The Ekmans waved until the big ship was so far out that they could no longer see Elias waving back to them. Marjatta had a little lump in her throat. He was a strange old man, but there was something very likable about him.

That afternoon the helicopter chartered by Mr. Magnussen took them out over the city, then headed toward

the Aland Islands, and the coast of Finland beyond.

The sun was lighting up the clouds over Finland, and the islands below looked like pieces of green carpet patterned with dwarf pine and juniper. Though they had only been away three unforgettable days, Marjatta and Mikael, as well as their parents, were glad to be heading back toward their island home.

"Would you want to go and work with Mr. Magnussen

and his ships, Mikael?" The question came from Marjatta. "He said he would find me work in one of his offices in Stockholm, when I am old enough."

Neither Mr. nor Mrs. Ekman said anything, but they waited anxiously to hear their son's reply.

Mikael looked down at the islands below. His eye caught a tiny spot of red, the sail of a fisherman's boat. Slowly he shook his head.

"It was nice to see a big city," he said slowly. "But . . . I think I would rather hear the wind in the trees, and saw wood for the winter fire, and go out after strömming."

"And you?" Mrs. Ekman asked Marjatta.

Marjatta said nothing; only shook her head. It had been exciting, and there would be much to talk about when school started again. But home was the islands—and Marjatta loved home.